WOLF RANCH: WILD

WOLF RANCH - BOOK 2

RENEE ROSE

VANESSA VALE

Wolf Ranch: Wild

Copyright © 2020 by Bridger Media and Wilrose Dream Ventures LLC

This is a work of fiction. Names, characters, places and incidents are the products of the author's imagination and used fictitiously. Any resemblance to actual persons, living or dead, businesses, companies, events or locales is entirely coincidental.

All rights reserved.

No part of this book may be reproduced in any form or by any electronic or mechanical means, including information storage and retrieval systems, without written permission from both authors, except for the use of brief quotations in a book review.

Cover design: Sarah Hansen / Okay Creations

Cover graphic:

1

Marina

My cell was ringing. The sky had opened up and was dumping buckets. I'd never seen it rain so hard. The wipers on my little rental barely worked, even on the highest setting. I was practically crawling down the back road, and it was going to take me hours to get to Audrey's.

"Shit," I said aloud, fumbling to grab the phone from my purse on the passenger seat. "Hello."

"Hello, Marina Thompson?"

A huge flash of lightning cut across the sky, and it illuminated the road in front of me. It wasn't dark yet, but it might as well have been midnight. I saw the road in front of me—or lack of it—and a split second later, I slammed on the brakes.

A car-rattling boom followed directly, which made me jump in my seat.

"Shit."

A huge river of water was cutting across the road.

"Hello?" the voice in the phone said.

I took a deep breath and stared out the window as best I could to the water that was blocking my way. It was too deep to cross.

"Oh my God. There's a river in the road… " I sighed. "Um, yes. This is Marina."

"I'm Janine Fitz in the bursar's office."

"Yes, hi. Sorry, I'm caught in a little bad weather." I added the last because the woman probably thought I was crazy.

"I wanted to inform you that the payment for fall semester has not come in," she said from somewhere dry and sunshiney at the university. "It was due last Monday."

I blinked, processed her words. Maybe I hadn't heard her right, for the rain was pounding on the car. "My father sends in a check for each semester."

That was pretty much all he did for me.

"It's not here. If we don't receive it promptly, we

will assume you are not attending for the upcoming school year."

"I'm attending," I said quickly. Another streak of lightning followed by a clap of thunder. "I am. Thank you for calling, and I'll follow through."

"Have a good day," she said.

"You, too." A good day? It was like the heavens had opened up in the middle of Montana.

I looked down at my phone in my hand. Sighed. "Dad, what's the deal?" I murmured as I quickly sent him a text about the missing money. I wasn't expecting a reply because he rarely did, so I tossed the cell onto the empty seat.

I glanced at the road again. I didn't think there was supposed to be a raging river out there. Or a bridge was missing. Either way, I wasn't going any further. This shouldn't be happening. I *had* to get to Wolf Ranch tonight.

"Not a chance," I mumbled.

There was nothing I could do about the tuition. Or the impassable road.

So I'd just go with it. Enjoy the here and now. The summer class was over, the exam done. I was on vacation. I pushed open the door and climbed out. Instantly, I was drenched. Maybe it was a stupid move getting soaked through, but I had to get out and see this crazy Montana storm in person.

Up close and personal.

Until an hour ago, the weather had been perfect. Sunny skies with big puffy clouds, mid-eighties. The storm had blown in quick, the Big Sky country living up to its name as I'd watched it roll in from the west, and I'd driven right into it.

The rain was chilly as it pounded my face, stuck my hair to my cheeks and neck, absorbed into my sneakers. I took a deep breath and tilted my face up to the sky. Only the sound of the rain and wind could be heard. No big city noises like car horns or sirens. No construction or dogs barking. Nothing but me and nature for miles and miles. I smiled.

I didn't realize how much I liked being out of the city until I was a time zone away. I could enjoy my break in Montana, starting with Audrey's wedding. I couldn't wait to meet the hot rodeo champ who'd lassoed her heart, the guy whose pics online were hot, hot, *hot*. I'd told Audrey once that I was vicariously living through her. I hadn't been lying.

My love life was non-existent. Sure, the guys in my department had asked me out, but none of them had done it for me. I had no idea what I was holding out for... some of them were handsome and nice. Smart. Funny. But they were boys.

I wanted a *man*. A real man. A manly man. A guy to take hold of my hair and drag me back to his cave. Oh, and maybe not for him to flake like the last one. Sticking would be good, too. Maybe I'd settle for not cheating.

God, the bar was getting lower and lower.

Still, I knew exactly what had been missing. What I was craving. Heat. Chemistry. Off the charts sizzle.

What Audrey had found with her cowboy.

I wasn't a virgin, but I might as well have been. The last guy I'd been with had traded me in for a newer model. That had been fun. Not. I wanted a guy who made me hot, where there was some kind of zing, like the lightning that lit up the sky. I craved it, and the dead batteries in my vibrator were proof of that.

I turned my face up and let the rain pelt my eyelids, my cheeks, my lips. And then I started to laugh. Took a deep breath, then another as I looked at the two-lane road in front of me. A creek had swelled over its banks and covered the roadway. The murky water rushed by, a tree branch or shrub ripped from the ground bobbed and moved downstream. Nature always won. Was always grander, bigger, stronger. It could always reduce my problems to insignificance. I picked up a rock and tossed it into the swift moving water to see how deep it was.

It instantly disappeared.

I laughed again. I wasn't getting across anytime soon, at least not on this road. All around me was nothing but prairie grass whipping in the wind. The nearest town was five miles back, although the term *town* was generous. It didn't even have a stoplight.

I could turn back and detour a different way, but the alternate route the GPS gave me took me three hours out of the way. And that was if those roads hadn't been flooded, too.

If I couldn't get to Wolf Ranch tonight, I wasn't in any hurry to get anywhere else. Might as well enjoy nature's ill-timed show. I climbed up onto a two-foot high stone and concrete marker by the side of the road to get a better look.

A pickup's headlights caught my attention, and I wobbled on the top of my perch. Because of the storm, I hadn't heard the engine until it stopped right behind my car. The door opened, and a large man climbed down and stalked toward me.

"You okay?" he called, concern lacing his voice.

I blinked the rain away, stared. Blinked again. Well, hell-*o*. Speaking of a real man.

The guy was huge, at least six-three or four. Solid muscle, as if he lifted little rental cars like mine for exercise, was barely concealed beneath a black t-shirt and cargo pants. He was instantly wet.

So was I, and not from the rain.

He stopped beside me, and even with me standing on the sign base, I stood only a foot above him. His hair was close-cropped and dark, although it was almost black now. He needed a shave, as if he'd lost his razor a few days ago. I bet he had a hairy chest.

Yum.

I laughed, nearly losing my balance again. "I'm fine. I was just having a look." I pointed toward the flooded road, but he didn't take his eyes off me.

He reached up and caught my elbow to steady me. A deep V crinkled his forehead. He was probably a decade older than me and wow... h.o.t., HOT.

"That water's deeper than you think," he said. His voice was deep, gruff and full of command. My body shuddered, not from the chill from the rain but in response to his words. "There's no way you'll get across."

Piercing dark eyes roved over me, stopping on my chest.

I looked down and realized my nipples were poking against my pale pink shirt which was now practically see-through. He didn't need x-ray vision to know I wasn't wearing a bra.

I turned my face to the rushing water. "I know. I just wanted to watch it for a minute." I turned my foot, and it slid a little on the slick surface.

His grip tightened on me. "Little girl, you're making me nervous. Hop down before I pull you down."

Little girl? I stared at him. I was so much smaller and definitely younger, but still. Those same bossy words out of another guy's mouth would have offended me. Somehow from him they sounded sexy. Virile. It probably had something to do with those bulging muscles in the arm holding me.

He reached for my waist, not waiting for me to comply. "Let's go." He lifted me easily to the ground, but kept his hands resting lightly on my waist. He looked around, as if searching for something, then back at me. His gaze roved over my face, dropped to my lips, then looked me square in the eyes.

"You're standing out here just to look? You're soaked through."

"So are you," I countered.

He tipped his head, like he wasn't used to being challenged, and I thought I saw the glimmer of a smile before he hid it. He bent his head to mine and inhaled sharply, nostrils flaring. I swore I heard him growl. His eyes widened like he was just as surprised by the sound as I was. He swore, but it got caught on the wind.

"Um... you're staring," I said finally, when he didn't look away. I didn't even think he blinked.

"Yeah."

Yeah? That was it?

Were we having a moment? Yes, I was definitely having a moment with a gorgeous manly-man stranger whose hands were still on me. I couldn't wait to tell Audrey.

I licked my lips, and I watched as his eyes followed the movement. He took another deep breath and growled again. He wasn't in a rush now to get me out of the rain. In fact...

"Um, you're still holding me."

His fingers tightened fractionally on my waist, the heat of his touch almost searing. He wasn't letting go. "I don't want you disappearing."

I frowned. "Well, I'm not going that way," I replied, with a tip of my head toward the rushing water. "Can you... um..." Whatever I was going to say fled when his thumbs began to slide back and forth over my wet shirt. It was as if he was touching my bare skin.

Heat flared. Need. A jolt of thrill. Of longing. Of... zing.

I broke the stare and looked him over. This close, he was huge. Broad, thickly muscled. I was in the middle of nowhere with a guy who could be the Incredible Hulk's brother. I should be afraid he might turn green and rip me limb from limb, but I wasn't. His intensity was insane. This close, I couldn't miss how dark his eyes were, with little flecks of lighter brown in them. All that chemistry I'd been thinking I'd never find? Wow. It was all right here. In his gaze. His touch. His very being. It was as if the lightning in the sky was coming off of us, the electricity and connection that powerful. I was surprised we didn't sizzle.

Yeah, I'd been reading too many of the romance novels Audrey had recommended. Maybe her whirlwind love affair with her rodeo cowboy had me yearning for my own adventures of the heart—or just the flesh. I'd just assumed I'd never feel... the heat from a guy. Crave a guy's touch. What his mouth and fingers could do. His cock, God. How he might thrust his hips and take me hard. This guy? I doubted he did sweet.

I barely noticed the rain hitting my face. I only felt his hands. Saw his deep stare. Heard his rough breath. He was just as affected by me as I was by him. "Out of the whole world, I find you here."

I frowned again. "What?" When he didn't reply, I asked, "Are you going to let me go?"

Slowly, he shook his head.

"Um... okay, well, I don't even know your name."

"Colton Wolf."

My mouth fell open.

This guy was Colton Wolf? Holy shit. There couldn't be two guys with that name in the middle of nowhere Montana, on a road headed toward Cooper Valley and Wolf Ranch. Audrey had told me about Boyd's brothers in one of our many gabfests. One lived on the ranch. Rob. The other was a Green Beret stationed on the east coast somewhere. Colton.

He wasn't on the east coast now. I had the insta-hots for my soon-to-be brother-in-law's brother. I exhaled, relieved. I wasn't lusting after a total stranger because not only was it dangerous and creepy, but Audrey'd kill me. She was fine with me having a one-night stand, but I didn't think she meant pick up a guy on the side of a deserted road and fuck him until I forgot my name. Regardless, I didn't want to climb a random man like a dang tree, no matter how hot he was. No, I wanted to climb Colton Wolf. And there was a lot to climb.

I'd complained to God in the car just a little while ago. Maybe the raging creek was fate. Destiny. Maybe I wasn't supposed to get to Wolf Ranch tonight. Maybe I was supposed to be in this guy's arms.

It seemed my bad luck had changed. Yet we were still standing here in the rain, and he didn't seem like he had any intention of moving.

I noticed he didn't ask my name. I cleared my throat. "You're right, we should get out of the rain."

Another slice of lightning, then thunder rumbled. He didn't even blink.

"Colton?"

His gaze had dropped to the side of my neck, and he was looking at me as if I were a buffet and he hadn't eaten in a week.

That was good, right? I wanted a guy to look at me like that. I wanted someone *ravenous* for me. Especially since I was that way in return.

But this was Colton Wolf. I knew of him, and I had to assume if he was driving to his family ranch too, he was returning for the wedding. That meant I had to assume he knew of me. Or at least knew that Audrey had a sister.

Crap. I was going to be a pseudo-little sister. I was far from related, but still, he'd already called me *little girl*. Would he have some kind of rule about not screwing the little sister? Yeah, I was thinking about having sex with him. By the look on his face, he wasn't interested in a make-out session.

He probably wouldn't want me if he knew who I was. Military guys sometimes got twisted up with honor and bro-codes.

I wasn't a bro, and while I had honor, I also had hormones that made me want this guy and *only* this guy. Tonight. It had to be tonight. Once we got to the ranch, and he knew who I was, everything would change.

"Don't you want to know my name?"

His eyes met mine. "It doesn't matter."

"It doesn't—" *Okay,* maybe he wanted a one-night stand after all. This could work. This could totally work. One night with the badass Green Beret. He was big, so I had to assume he was proportional... everywhere. My pussy clenched at the possibility.

Running a hand over his face, he wiped the rain away, at least for a second. It looked like he had a scar through his eyebrow. There was a slice of dark hair missing, but I didn't see a healed wound.

The wind kicked up, the gale pushing me forward and closer to him.

He breathed deep, and I watched as his nostrils flared again. Every line of his body tensed, and his hand still on my hip tightened more. His eyes seemed to glow in the headlights. He looked... wild.

Lightning lit up his features in stark contrast, and I counted.

One, one thousand.

Two, one thousand.

Boom. I shot forward into his arms. Okay, I needed to move this along. He seemed to be fine staring at me, holding me to him and... oddly enough, breathing me in. But damn, his strong arms felt good wrapped around me. Where I was cold, he was warm.

"Easy," he murmured right by my ear. "You're safe with me. I promise."

My heart skipped a beat, then practically pounded out of my chest as I listened to him take another deep breath.

"I know." I lifted my face and beamed up at him.

"Fuck me," he muttered.

Did he say *fuck me* as in I should fuck him? *Yes,*

please. Slowly, I shook my head. "Um, I think *you're* supposed to fuck *me.*"

One dark brow winged up. "What are you saying?"

I smirked in the rain at the press of his cock—his huge, long, thick cock—press against me. "I think I made it pretty clear."

His gaze roved over my face again, as if memorizing it. "Little girl, you are pure damage."

I dragged my lower lip through my teeth. My small breasts pressed up against his ribs, my hands were on his rock-hard abs.

"The creek won't go down for hours after the storm's blown through," he explained. "There's a motel in the last town."

Dark, tawdry thoughts instantly filled my head. His hands moved to my shoulders, but his gaze dropped to my breasts again, like he was thinking about cupping them.

If he did, he'd find out they were small, only an A-cup, but my nipples were hard enough to cut glass. I had to hope I was enough for a brawny guy like him. I might be small, but I wouldn't break, and while I hadn't had tons of sex—okay, barely any—I had pretty naughty thoughts.

Suddenly, I wasn't cold. His scent caught on the

wind. Soap or something spicy, but beneath it... man.

"You need to get out of those wet clothes," he almost snarled.

So do you, my friend.

Would he help me undress? Lift my long-sleeved t-shirt over my head? Would he work my leggings down over my hips taking my thong with it? Would he pat every inch of my skin dry with a towel, or would it evaporate away when he kissed me?

The road in front of us was impassable. We'd spend the night in the motel he mentioned, but if I had my way, we wouldn't do much sleeping.

2

VANILLA AND CINNAMON. That was her delectable scent. She was breathtaking. Perfect.

Fuck me. It was as if an IED had gone off right in front of me. Ripping me open, destroying the man I had been and forcing my wolf to heal me into something new. Because he had, knowing she was my mate.

Yeah, I was a fucking poet now, but it was as if the clouds broke open and a beam of sunshine... shit.

I'd caught one whiff of her sweet smell mingled

even in the rain, and I recognized her as mine. The One. I'd stilled and time seemed to have stopped. The slip of a female who'd been recklessly standing out in the rain staring at a fucking swollen creek was it for me. My wolf, who'd been restless lately—almost the past two years—perked right up. Snapped and snarled at me to get my attention. As if I'd needed that to know.

She. Was. The. One.

She'd asked me if I was going to let her go. I'd shaken my head. There was no fucking way I was letting her out of my sight ever again. I'd been in the military for over a decade. Done three tours in the worst hell holes on Earth. I'd also been all over the world. Met, and slept with, countless women hoping my wolf would be happy. Sure, my dick had gotten a workout, and I'd been able to empty my balls without using my hand, but they'd been empty fucks. Shallow—although I'd ensured the woman walked away well satisfied—but meaningless.

Now? Here in a fucking summer storm? Her? My dick was rock hard. I was eager to learn everything about her, and my wolf wanted to bite and claim her. *Now.*

I'd had to let her go, let her get in her car and follow her back to town. I stayed right on her tail, and if she even so much as changed her mind and decided to drive right on past the motel, I'd have cut her off and blocked her way just like the fucking creek.

Thank fuck, she hadn't, which meant all the signs that had been pinging off of her better than a satellite were in sync with mine.

This was happening. *We* were a go. Mission Make-Her-Mine was on. There was no way she knew I was a shifter, but by morning, she'd know a whole hell of a lot about me. What I could do with my hands. My mouth. She'd learn the size of my dick and how it would be a tight fit in her little pussy. Her mouth... or fuck, her tight ass.

After checking in at the front desk, I unlocked the door to the motel room and stood out in the rain to usher her in. She was so beautiful, even dripping wet, her clothes clinging to her slight curves. Her hair was a medium shade of brown, but I figured it would be lighter when dry. Long. Curly, even.

I thought back to seeing her standing up on the stone pillar getting soaked. I'd stopped immediately when I saw a car at the swollen river, then I got a glimpse of her. A crazy thing out in the storm. But when I'd actually gotten up close to her—after I'd caught her scent and taken in that ripe body—my life had changed forever.

I remembered my dad talking about how it was when a shifter found his female. Instantaneous. Like lightning. Life altering. Permanent.

I'd believed him but doubted everyone found their mate. I was at the end of my chances, the moon madness affecting me more and more. But he'd been right although it seemed my wolf was set on a reckless little thing. Fuck, the thought of her getting swept away in the raging water made him want to howl.

Christ, even now that I knew she was safe for the night, I wanted to spank her ass pink for scaring the wolf in me like that.

Yeah, I wanted to get my hands all over that shapely ass of hers.

Fate knew, I wanted to take it all. I wanted to peel that pale pink t-shirt off her wet body and get my mouth on one of those hard little nipples showing through. I wanted to find out if she had panties on under those leggings because I sure as hell hadn't seen a line. I wanted to wrap my palms around those sexy thighs and pull them around to ride my waist. She was so small, I doubted she'd even be able to cross her ankles.

Those leggings showed every glorious curve, and her ass was so very spankable. She was nothing like my usual type, and yet she sparked my basest desires. I went for a sturdier kind of woman. The kind who could take a hard, rough fucking and not whine about it. That's what was in me.

This one I could snap in two with the flick of my hand. It didn't make sense that my wolf wanted to claim her. But he did. I did. I wanted to see my handprints on her skin, make her gloriously aware of our difference in size and strength. Watch those eyes widen in shock when I took her hard, then soften and blur when she submitted to the pleasure I'd give her.

She stared up at me, not seeming to notice I was right on the edge. She was beautiful—wild hair, dark eyes, pale skin. I couldn't fucking wait to make her turn that megawatt smile on me again.

I fought the urge to toss her over my shoulder and carry her over to the bed like a conquering Viking. I was already worried she'd be scared of me. I was a big guy and a stranger. She was a twig that could blow away in the wind. Definitely too trusting. Maybe I'd spank her ass for that, too. My mate was willing to go off and fuck a stranger? My wolf snarled.

Yeah, a spanking was definitely in order. I popped her on the ass as she came into the room before I could stop myself.

She gave a little gasp that made my dick go rock hard and looked over her shoulder at me. I expected her to be angry, and I'd deserve it, but her eyes went smoky, her pouty lips parted. She fucking liked it. It got her going.

She was temptation personified, and my control hung by a thread. Finally, she was here. Scented. Identified. *Mine.*

"You always go to motel rooms with strangers?" I asked, trying to keep my voice calm, but it was fucking hard thinking about her doing this with anyone else.

Her eyes narrowed. "Do you?"

I wasn't bringing up past women because they were just that. My past. She was my future, and I wasn't fucking it up with words.

Her eyes took on a guarded quality, and her voice slowed when she said, "You said I was safe with you."

"You are," I replied quickly, cutting off her fears before they even started. "You're a reckless one, though. Maybe in need of a spanking."

Her mouth fell open, but her eyes also widened.

I couldn't miss the way her pupils dilated, and when I took a deep breath... fuck.

She was aroused. I could scent her pussy from here.

"You like that idea." I didn't state it as a question because I knew the answer. I didn't want her to be embarrassed... or lie. Then she'd really get a spanking and not a fun kind.

She looked away, gave a slight shrug. "There's nothing wrong with a woman going after what she wants," she snapped.

"Good girls like to get fucked, too. No question," I said. "As long as you get it with me."

"That's why I'm here," she replied, her gaze dropping to the front of my wet pants. I was hard. It couldn't be hidden. When her mouth fell open because she couldn't miss the thick length going down the inside of my thigh, my wolf preened. Yeah, that was all for her.

Except... I should put her in her own room, ensure she was safely tucked away until the road was open. That would be the gentlemanly thing to do. Usually, I was one, but right here, right now?

No fucking way. There was no doubt she was a good girl in need of a hard, thorough fucking. My wolf snarled at the possibility of her having come across someone else on the side of the road. If we'd missed her, even by a few minutes...

But we hadn't.

She was mine, and I'd give her whatever she wanted, especially if it involved my dick. All my debating dropped away when she just stood there in the center of the room, water dripping from her. Nipples hard, eyes glued to my dick... it was as if she was waiting for it. For *me*.

And then I forgot all honor. Forgot my intention to not scare her. Not to come on too strong. She was here willingly. She'd had plenty of opportunity to change her mind. The way she ogled me, she had no plans to do so.

She might not know she was my mate, but I'd sure as fuck show her.

Two steps, and I was on her, sliding my hands around her waist, tugging up the hem of her soaked t-shirt. "Let me help you with this," I murmured, my voice three times as deep as normal.

I went slowly, in case she resisted, but she still didn't. Yeah, she was right here with me. The little siren kept her gaze locked on mine as she lifted her arms over her head. I pulled the shirt off and let out a low curse.

Her breasts were small and perky, with dusky

rose nipples that tilted up. They wouldn't fill my palms, but she also didn't need to wear a bra. I'd be fucking hard all the time knowing she was bare beneath her shirts. She stepped closer to me, her hands sliding under my soaked t-shirt to brush my abs. A ripple of pleasure ran through me, stronger than anything I'd felt before.

I'd spent the last twelve years searching for my mate, hoping I'd find her before I went moon mad. Why fate had made me wait until I was almost lost to it, I had no idea. Living on base was like living in a big city. There was no privacy. Nowhere to roam. Hell, nowhere to run as a wolf. I now knew she was the only one who could alleviate my growing frenzy to claim, mark and breed. It had affected my performance on base, making my ever growing need to shift, roam and run mess with my abilities to command. That was fucking bad because when I couldn't command, my men died.

Boyd's wedding had been the excuse I'd given for taking leave and returning to Montana. In truth, I needed the space the ranch offered to run hard, to deal with the madness that had been hounding me. And fuck if I didn't just find my mate a hundred miles from home, in the impossibly cute, fragile, *young* body of a human.

Because I knew the moment I caught her scent.

My wolf stood up and howled, *this one.*

She was my mate, but I didn't even know her name. Right now, with my mouth watering to suck on her gorgeous nipples, it wasn't important. I'd know her anywhere from her scent alone. In comparison, her name was trivial.

I dipped my head to catch her lips, tasting her. "You want this, sweetness? You want my hands on this hot-as-sin body of yours?"

"*Yes.*"

I was comforted by the fact that she didn't hesitate with her answer. I might be a one-night stand for her, but she trusted me.

"You sure?" I wrapped my hands around her ribs, brushing her nipples with my thumbs. "Because I'm not sure I can be respectful once I get you naked, sweetness." I walked her backward until she hit the wall, and I pinned her there, claiming her mouth as I pinched both nipples.

She licked between my lips, and the tether on my control snapped. I slid my hands down to close them around her asscheeks, lifting her legs to wrap around my waist. My hard cock punched out against the sturdy cotton of my cargo pants. I ground into the notch between her legs to ease the need.

"I-I'm not looking for respectful." I loved her breathless reply.

Her arms twined around my neck, and she kissed like her life depended on it. I prided myself on staying cool, calm and collected in every situation, but she had my heart pounding, my control slipping. My wolf was in fucking heaven.

"Show me," she whispered.

I thrust between her legs again. "Show you what, little girl?" I growled.

"I'm ready to be disrespected."

I threw back my head and laughed with surprise. Cute. She was so fucking cute.

She tossed her head, her wet hair sending droplets flying through the room. "Let's do this."

I shouldn't.

I definitely shouldn't.

Especially not the way I fucked. When it came to sex, I was the furthest thing from vanilla there was. And she was as fresh-faced as a flower.

A not-so-innocent flower who was grinding over my cock like she needed it inside her.

I carried her to the bed and dropped her on her back, pulling off my t-shirt with a one-handed arc, and it landed on the floor behind me with a wet splat.

Her gaze traveled over my shoulders and chest, down my arms. "Mmm."

"You like what you see, little girl?"

She wriggled that cute ass of hers on the bed. "Definitely."

"You have no idea what you're in for." I grasped the waistband of her leggings and tugged. A miniscule pair of panties came down with them, and a wolf growl rocketed out of my throat. She was neatly trimmed and had the sweetest pussy I'd ever fucking seen.

Her belly shivered in on a breath. *And then she fucking spread her legs.*

"Oh, you're a bad girl," I said, taking in every pink inch of her. I dove between those parted legs, pushing her thighs wider and licking into her. She let out a cry of pleasure that nearly made me jizz in my pants like a teenager, especially when her hips jacked up, knees clamping around my ears.

Not only could I breathe in her sweet scent, but her taste burst on my tongue. While her skin was chilled from the rain, her pussy was hot. Wet. Dripping.

"Uh uh," I scolded, pushing her knees wide. "Keep 'em open for me, little girl, or you'll be punished."

Christ. I didn't even know what made me say it. Yeah, I liked to dominate but only with women who I knew for certain liked it. I didn't even know her name let alone what got her off.

I licked through her folds, and she cried out again, knees slamming closed. "I can't help it!" she gasped. "It feels so good."

Maybe I knew what revved her engine after all.

I reached up and gently slapped the side of her breast, then pinched her nipple as punishment.

"Oh my God," she moaned, pushing her sweet pussy into my face, knees splaying wide.

She liked her punishment.

Noted and fucking celebrated. But of course, she did. She was my goddamn mate. Nature wouldn't send me an incompatible female. No, I'd have one who was as wild as I was. She was fucking perfect.

I gave her more of my tongue, licking her from anus to clit. She screamed, pulling on my ears, her ass rolling up off the bed. I had to hope the walls of the motel weren't too thin because those staying in the other rooms were going to hear her pleasure all night long. I didn't care. My wolf didn't care either. It meant I was taking good care of our woman, and the whole motel could know it.

The way she thrashed and dripped all over my

chin, you'd think she'd never been eaten properly before. Well, I was going to take care of that. I wasn't sure if I should be angry that the men she'd been with before were selfish pricks or woefully inadequate in the sack or thrilled that she'd find out the depth of her passion with only me.

That made me focus even more on the task, and I pinned her pelvis down to the bed. "*Down*, little, girl. Be good, and I'll make it last."

"Oh, please," she whimpered, sounding needy as fuck. She undulated her hips, pushing against my mouth.

Fates, was she already trembling? Already ready for release? How is that possible? She was so open, so willing, so responsive. It made my wolf growl with the need to protect her.

From everybody but me.

I made my tongue flat and licked the length of her, then found the little nubbin of her clit and pushed the hood back, working to get my lips around it and suck.

She pulled my ears again, pressing my face into her juicy flesh. I shifted my position and screwed my thumb into her. She was tight—so fucking tight—but soaking wet, her flesh plumped and welcoming. She moaned a desperate keening sort of sound. I pumped my thumb and let my middle finger burrow between her cheeks to settle over her anus.

Another scream. Her tight little rosebud clenched under the pad of my finger, and I massaged it, applying a little pressure to see if she'd let me in.

"Oh my God. Oh my God. This is crazy," she chanted, still trying to rip my ears off my head to bring me closer. I withdrew my hand to spit on my fingers then returned them to the same configuration. This time, when I massaged her back hole, I got in.

She let out a sort of shocked vocalization. A long "aaaaaah" that ended with several short staccato tones. I had no doubt that was the first time she'd had something in her ass. The way she was responding, it wouldn't be the last. It suddenly became my life's goal to get those sounds out of her on a nightly basis. Or daily.

Screw the Green Berets. My new assignment was making my mate scream.

What could be more important?

I worked my fingers slowly, pushing my thumb in deep as I withdrew the finger in her ass, then reversing the motion. All the while, I sucked, licked, flicked and nipped her swollen clit, driving her to a mad frenzy.

Sweet little human.

She never knew what hit her.

She had no idea what she was in for when she slipped me the tongue.

Her legs thrashed around me as she squirmed and panted and mewled. I switched up my technique and fucked both holes at the same time with quick, short thrusts.

Her voice rose so loud everyone in the packed motel definitely heard her, and fuck if that didn't make my wolf preen. Still, she was fighting the orgasm, which would make it all the bigger when she finally let go.

I broke the suction of my lips over her clit and flipped her to her belly, my fingers still filling both holes. Then I slapped her ass, a cherry red handprint appearing instantly.

That was all it took. One spank and she came, both holes squeezing up tight around my fingers. I slowed the thrusts and changed back to the alternating rhythm, applying a lighter spank to the same cheek, then another. Fuck, she was a sight. Her thighs stuck out straight beneath her, muscles tight, ass cheeks squeezing while she continued to come and come.

I squeezed a handful of her pretty ass and shook

it. "That's one version of disrespectful," I told her. "I have a whole catalog of other ones, if you'd like me to trot them out."

She moaned into the covers. I slowly eased my fingers out and sat back to take in her gorgeous form. She lay limp and spent, still catching her breath. Her hair hung in damp sections over her slender shoulder. My handprints bloomed pink on her pale skin. Marked.

I got up and washed my hands in the tiny bathroom. When I came back, she twisted her shoulders to look at me from under dark lashes. So. Fucking. Beautiful. I climbed on the bed and stroked a hand down her back.

"Wow," she murmured.

I smirked and fell down on her, pinning her wrists beside her head, straddling her ass. "Bite off more than you could chew, little girl?"

Her face was turned to the side against the bedcovers, and she smiled, looking over her shoulder. "What makes you think that?"

I leaned down and nipped her ear. "Just checking." I straightened. My cock ached for release, but I could wait. I was so fascinated by my mate, by this unique human female my wolf had chosen for us.

But the idea of this activity being her normal

gnawed at me some more. Was she reckless with her safety? With men? The protector in me nearly went wild with those thoughts. "Please tell me you don't make this a common practice."

Her brows dipped. "What? Hooking up with strange men in motel rooms?" Tension appeared in her limbs, where they'd been limp before, as if she just realized what she'd done.

I didn't want her to think I was judging. Or slut shaming. But I was ready to kill any man who'd been here before me or—fate forbid—would come after.

I'd plowed into this so fast because I recognized her as mine, but she didn't know a thing about me. Which scared the fuck out of me. And very little on this Earth scared me. As a shifter, I was pretty much invincible, and I'd been involved in some dangerous shit. Until now. Now, my heart could be destroyed, and she was the only one who could do it.

"I just wanna think this is something special. A one-off." I arched a brow. "Is it?"

She jerked her shoulder with what looked like irritation, and I immediately released her, moving off and setting her free. Scaring her was definitely not part of my plan.

"Why?" she demanded, defensiveness lacing her tone. "I'm not used to men sticking around."

I caught her chin and turned her face toward me. I'd offended her, and I needed to put her at ease. Even thought she'd lumped me in with these other men she mentioned.

"Come on, throw me a bone, little girl. Can't you tell when a guy is fishing for a compliment? This is where you tell me I'm special."

Since when did I want a *fucking* bone from a woman? Since *her*. Fuck.

She relaxed, a reluctant smile tugging her lips. "It's a one-off," she admitted, and my wolf stopped the internal growling. "My sex life for the last three years has been pathetic. The last guy ditched me for my lab partner. So a sex life? Non-existent—but I'm not a virgin," she clarified.

That made me want to smash something, knowing another guy had been there before me and been a dick about it. But I couldn't be a hypocrite.

She looked me over, took in my bare chest. "I've been dreaming of a man who knows what he's doing. Then you showed up... all ready to rescue me from the raging river." She rolled to fully face me, that spirited smile stretching her lips. "I deserve a fling."

A fling, where she couldn't be ditched for a newer model because it was short lived.

It seemed I'd finger fucked her into forgetting about that douche canoe because that smile was megawatt. I was a fucking goner. This was more than a fling, but now wasn't the time to talk. Taking the smile as an invitation, I covered one small breast with my palm and squeezed. "Happy to oblige, sweetness."

3

Marina

"Is this a first for you, too?" I shouldn't have asked. I wasn't sure I wanted to hear the answer.

I knew Boyd was quite the player, and Audrey'd had a hard time initially trusting he really liked her. If he looked anything like Colton, I could see why. This man was Gerard Butler gorgeous. I'd be smart to assume he was as much of a lady's man as his brother, which meant I had to fuck carefully, not do something stupid like get my heart involved. I was used to men loving and leaving, or maybe not loving at all. If I were smart, I'd expect it from Colton Wolf, too. He was a Green Beret, here in

Montana only for the wedding. He wasn't looking to settle down. Hell, I doubted he was actually *looking*.

Still, I found my heart beat faster waiting for his answer.

"I'm not a virgin either."

I rolled my eyes. *Duh.* "Your mad skills gave that away."

He gazed at me, his expression clouding before he answered. "Little girl, I do not make a habit of picking up drenched women by the side of the road and seducing them."

"I thought I was seducing you," I countered, biting my lip. I was all soft and pliant from that insane orgasm.

He studied me, eyes crinkled and warm. "So you were."

"What *do* you make a habit of, Colton?"

He shook his head. "Not this." He bent to brush his lips between my breasts. I shivered, every nerve-ending still sensitized to his touch.

Gawd. We hadn't even had actual sex yet, and I was pretty sure Colton Wolf had ruined me for other men. I'd wanted adventures in bed. He'd definitely delivered, and it only felt like the beginning. As if he was giving me a chance to recover.

I reached for the button on his pants. His cock had tented the fabric from the moment we came in the room, and it must be getting painful for him. And yet, I noticed he backed right off when I wanted him to. So he *was* respectful.

Very.

Which made his dominant manhandling all the more delicious. And the spanking? My butt still tingled... and so did my pussy. Oh. My. God. "Ready to show me another version of disrespectful?" I purred.

In a strange trick of the light, his eyes took on an amber glow, and a low growl rumbled from inside his chest like he was ready to devour me.

Yes, *please.*

He pounced on me, straddling my waist again, this time with me on my back, and manacled my wrists with one hand above my head. His pants were wet and cool, but it felt good against my heated skin. "You like it rough, little girl?"

"Yes," I answered immediately. Did I? How in the hell would I know? But I was sure of my answer. If he gave it rough, that was how I wanted it. I wanted it all.

He tilted his head to the side. "You're a wild

thing, aren't you?" Admiration poured from his voice, his gaze—like he found me fascinating.

"Am I?" If only he knew how very dull my life really was. An engineering student who liked to bake. Someone who needed to visit her newly-found half-sister in Montana to let go and have a good time because life in LA was a dud.

But right now, I got to be wild with Colton Wolf. I got to have wild sex in a motel room with a stranger I knew was safe. I was going to milk this for everything I could get out of it.

I put on my best bedroom eyes and arched my breasts up toward his face as an invitation. "Do you have a condom?"

My experience may have been limited, but I wasn't stupid. Wild flings in Montana were not supposed to have unintended consequences, even if the stranger was Colton Wolf. And with Audrey being an Ob/Gyn, she'd kill me if I didn't practice what she preached.

"I'll protect you, sweetness. Don't worry about that."

I'll protect you.

Interesting choice of words. Not, *I'll wear protection.* Or, *Yes, I have condoms.* As if he took pride in keeping me safe from his sperm or diseases or anything else that came my way.

It made sense. Colton was a military hero. He dedicated his life to Americans' safety. He probably gloried in any opportunity to protect a woman. It made me even more sure I'd done the right thing by not telling him my name. He was a man of honor, even though he was pinning me naked to a bed. He lived by rules and codes. I didn't think he'd be so quick to spend the night in a motel room with me if he knew I was Boyd's soon-to-be little sister.

It probably messed with his plans for a wild night and nothing more.

He scraped his teeth over my nipple, then sucked it until I felt the answering tug in my core. What would he do with me, exactly? A flood of torrid images flashed through my mind. Would he tie me up? Put me on my knees to suck his dick? I loved the fact that he was in charge. There was none of the awkward figuring stuff out I'd experienced with partners before. He wasn't a high school or college boy.

He was all man.

I twisted my wrists in his hand. Not because I wanted to get free, more because I wanted to feel his strength. "I'll bet you're good with knots," I observed.

"Knots?" His lips twitched and he looked up at me. "You want me to tie you up, little girl?"

I both wanted it and was terrified of it at the same time. What if I hated it, and then I was trapped? What if it hurt?

Also, I didn't want to be calling the shots here. There was freedom in just letting him run the show.

"I want..." Hmm. I didn't know what I wanted, beyond that I wanted a sexual experience unlike any I've ever had.

He dropped his head to my other nipple and flicked his tongue. "What do you want, sweetness?"

"Um..."

"I know what you like," Colton said, like he'd arrived at a decision.

Thank God. I felt relieved but didn't understand how. "You do?"

He rolled me to my belly, then lifted my hips in the air, slapping my ass with a resounding smack.

"Ow!" I protested but then wiggled my hips. It stung, but a good kind of sting. A give-me-more kind of pain.

He stroked his hand over my smarting flesh, soothing away the tingle, then slapped my offended cheek again.

"Mmm." He rubbed between my legs, and I

could tell my folds were flooded with moisture. "That made you so wet, little girl. Your ass is already pink from those swats I gave you earlier. I think you like a little pain with your pleasure."

He slapped the other cheek, not as hard.

"Mmm," I agreed, wiggling my hips. I'd never been spanked before. Ever. I had no idea it got me hot.

He gave a sharper smack. "Use your words, sweetness. You want more?"

I waggled my ass. "Yes, please."

"Good girl."

He peppered my ass with light spanks—the fun kind. Not too hard, but enough to make me gasp and pant. The warmer my butt got, the hotter the fire in my core. I knew I was dripping all over his fingers. I'd never been this wet before. Nothing in my limited experience—either with a guy or self-loving—had wound my crank like this. I burned everywhere and nothing, *nothing*, would ease that flame but his cock inside me. I just knew it.

"P-please," I gasped, dropping to my forearms. I rubbed my aching nipples over the sheets.

He slapped a little harder. "What do you need, little girl?"

"I want you in me," I pleaded, then bit my lip. I was close to coming just from this alone.

His chuckle was dark. "That's where I wanna be, too, sweetness." He slid his fingers through my slick folds making me moan, then gave another spank.

I watched over my shoulder as he freed his sizable erection. Oh. My. God.

"Like what you see?" he asked, gripping the base in a tight fist and stroking. He was thick and long, the broad head an angry color. Pre-cum beaded at the slit at the top, and I licked my lips.

Shit. Would that fit? Could I take all those inches? He ripped open a condom packet with his teeth and rolled it on. And on. And on.

Should I warn him how tight I'd be? No, I wouldn't want him to know how inexperienced I was. I feared he'd be the type who'd think he was taking advantage of my innocence although after the way he ate me out, I wasn't all that innocent any longer.

My pussy clenched. Maybe it wouldn't be that bad. After all, I'd used my vibe recently, and I was wet enough to get him to slide in.

He dragged the head of his cock through my swollen folds, and I moaned at the gratification.

Yes. This was exactly what I needed.

No matter how big he was.

He gathered my wet hair in his fist and used it to lift and turn my head. "I wanna see your face, sweetness. You keep it turned like that so I can watch you take every inch."

Oh, dayum. He could dirty-talk.

With his other hand, he slapped my ass.

"Ohh," I moaned, clenching down, then sighing as the heat spread.

He pushed the tip in. I gulped at how he was opening me up. Wow. Yep, he was big. But it also felt so right. Like delicious satisfaction. I arched and pushed my hips back to work him in deeper.

"Greedy little thing, aren't you? It's a snug fit, though. I'm gonna go slow to start, sweetness." He eased in another inch, then retreated.

I let out a moan with my exhale. So good. My walls rippled, adjusting to taking so much. My vibrator had nothing on this monster.

Colton let out a groan of his own when he plowed a little deeper. He reached down and brushed some hair back from my face. "I'm gonna pound you so hard when I finally get in."

His words caused me to shove back and take him deeper.

He cursed and gripped my hips with both hands, plunging in the rest of the way.

I gasped, my eyes momentarily rolling back in my head with pleasure as he bottomed out. "Oh!"

He stayed where he was, seated to the hilt and gave a slow roll of his hips. I felt the brush of his pants against my hot bottom, and the idea that I was completely bare while he wasn't was so fucking hot. As if he couldn't wait another second to strip before he got inside me.

"Mmm."

He eased out and in with micro-pumps, bumping my ass with his loins each time, his balls tapping my clit. "Oh God," I moaned.

He slowed but increased the range. Not full strokes, but half-strokes.

I fisted the bedcovers and pushed back, spread my knees more, hollowed my back.

He leaned over me, setting his hands beside my head, so he could kiss along my spine. "You are just the tastiest little hu—woman," he growled approvingly. "You like taking my big cock?"

"God, yes."

He pushed back up, gripped her hips and thrust hard.

My inner thighs already trembled. My brain

power took a nose-dive. I surrendered, letting sensation take over. The feeling of his cock filling me, stretching me. His fingers digging in. The sound of his ragged breath and my own cries and gasps. The nudge of his thighs against mine, the tickle of his hairs against my skin. His scent—clean and masculine. And, of course, the tang of sex.

"You want it harder?" Colton rasped.

"Yes."

The answer to every question of his would be yes. As long as he was offering more.

He plunged in harder, nearly sending my head into the headboard. He caught my shoulder and braced me for his thrusts, jackhammering into me. It was good. So good.

Like one hundred times better than my favorite-chocolate-mousse-cake good.

Stars danced before my eyes. I was hurtling toward a finish when he slowed down and pulled out.

"No," I whimpered. "Colton, please."

He flipped me over and pulled my ankles up over his shoulders. He was so big my butt was off the bed. I could do nothing but take what he gave me, which was every hard inch. When he entered me in this position, I nearly screamed. His thrusts were even more intense. So good.

I would shatter soon. Any moment.

"Hold your breasts," he grunted. His voice was deep and raspy and broken.

I cupped them. "Like this?"

He nodded. "Play with them."

I moaned as I squeezed my own nipples, doing it more for him than me, but receiving all the reward, nonetheless.

"You keep making those sexy sounds, little girl, I'm not gonna last."

"Come, Colton," I told him, watching the way his muscles tensed, then relaxed. His jaw was clenched, as if he were gritting his teeth. I was so freaking ready, and I wasn't even touching my clit. I'd never been able to come without that kind of stimulation. Then again, I'd never been pounded by a monster dick.

The light caught his eyes again, making them look amber, and he let out an animal-like roar. "Fuck!" He pumped harder and faster, making the entire bed bounce and hit the wall with a steady wham-wham-wham. It hurt but felt good all at once.

The people in the room next door pounded on the wall, and I giggled as Colton roared again and came. He parted my legs and dropped down between them, hovering over me as he thrust so deep, I thought he'd split me in two. His face contorted with his climax. Another thrust. A third. On the fourth, he shoved deep and stayed, and I came, too, like I was waiting for that moment. Which, I guess, biologically speaking, my body was.

I wrapped my legs around his back and rubbed my clit up and down against him as my internal muscles spasmed with release, trying to keep it going as long as possible.

Hol. E. Crap.

I was a changed woman. Or maybe I finally became a woman, I didn't know.

All I knew was that nothing in this world would ever be as good as sex with Colton Wolf. I could barely catch my breath. My bottom was sore against the sheets, my pussy had just taken a pounding. I ached in all the right places but felt soooo good.

I couldn't help but laugh.

That was what I'd been missing? He was still inside me, and I wanted it again. The question was would I ever stop wanting what I was realizing only he could give me.

COLTON

MATE.

Mate.

My wolf kept crooning it as I caught my breath. As the blindness that the incredible orgasms brought about receded.

Yeah, I know, buddy. I'm on it. Just didn't want to mark her before I found out her name.

Or had her consent. She might like me taking charge, but she'd wanted it. Claiming her tonight? Probably not.

I dipped to savor her mouth, my cock still buried deep in her snug little channel. I eased back and slammed in again, hard.

Fates, I should've given it a rest. She had to be tender after the pounding I'd given her, but I couldn't seem to help myself. My eyes rolled back in my head with pleasure every time her muscles squeezed my dick. Her vanilla and cinnamon scent was up in my nostrils, doing crazy things to my brain. To my body. To have her taste on my tongue… shit.

I looked down at my little mate. Her eyes were closed, but the corner of her mouth was tipped up.

Blonde hair was a tangle around her head. She looked well fucked—hell, my dick was still inside her. Sated. My wolf was pleased with himself to make her this way. So was I.

She thought this was a fling though. A little fun while waiting out a storm. A stranger fuck. Well, that was fucking wrong. I'd have to disabuse her of that notion soon. Telling her I was her fucking mate wasn't the smartest move either. Tomorrow, I'd find out where she was headed and follow her there. Make sure she got home safe, and then make sure she knew I'd be by that evening to pick her up for our first date.

Hell, maybe she could even be my date to Boyd's wedding. No, not could. *Would.*

I smiled, liking that idea. Nothing would make me more proud than to introduce my mate to my brothers.

But right now, I needed to take care of her needs. And they may not all include service from my dick.

I broke the kiss and eased out of her. While I didn't want to pull out of her tight, hot pussy... ever, I needed to ditch the condom.

"I'll be right back, sweetness."

I disposed of the latex barrier, then cracked a

bottle of water I'd bought at the front desk and brought it to her.

She sat up, so fucking gorgeous with her glassy eyes and swollen lips, completely uninhibited. Her cheeks were flushed from sex, her nipples hard little points from sucking on them. My whiskers left soft burns on her silky flesh. I couldn't see the insides of her thighs, but I knew they were there. While my cum was inside the condom in the trash, she was fucking marked.

She drank thirstily, and I kicked myself for not offering it sooner.

"What else do you need, beautiful? Are you hungry? Or do you need something warm to drink?"

She shook her head, her lids drooping. "That was... wow. I'm ready to crash."

I pulled down the covers and slid into the bed beside her. "Crash away, little girl. I'll protect you. If you wake up and your pussy needs more attention, I'll take care of you."

She rolled up against my chest and let me wrap an arm around her. A leg was tossed over mine, and her pussy pressed into my thigh. Fuck, I was hard again.

Her soft lips found the hollow of my throat, and she kissed it. "Thank you, Colton."

I kissed the top of her head. It struck me that with all the women I'd satisfied in all the years, I'd never dropped a kiss on any woman's head. It was an affectionate gesture, not a sexual one.

My arms tightened around her. This one was special. No, more than fucking special. She was perfect. She was mine.

Soon she'd know that, too.

4

Marina

I HAD no idea what woke me, but I looked around, not remembering where I was. The room was dark, illuminated only through the exterior light that slipped in through the sliver in the curtains. The motel.

It was the hard body I was sprawled upon like a blanket that had everything coming back in a rush. Colton stirred beneath me, his skin almost hot against my chest. His legs stirred, bringing the one I was practically straddling up and against my core. I was sore from earlier, but being with him like this made me eager for round two.

"No. Don't," he murmured, his head moving from side to side.

I lifted my head off his chest and looked up at him. I could make out his features, the tenseness of his jaw. I felt the way his body beneath mine went from relaxed in sleep to taut.

"No," he said again, this time his voice cutting through the stillness of the night.

I ran my hand over him, touching all of him that I could to try and soothe him. "Colton," I murmured, then repeated it when he didn't respond.

All at once, he startled, then blinked. "What?" he said, his voice gravelly. His hand, which had been resting on my lower back, stroked up and down, then cupped my butt.

"I think you were having a nightmare."

With his other hand, he rubbed it over his face. "Sorry."

I pressed a kiss to his chest, felt his heat, the beating of his heart against my lips. "Want to tell me about it?"

He sighed and was quiet so long, I thought he wouldn't answer. "Too many deployments. Afghanistan."

I could only imagine what he saw, the horrors he'd had to face. I'd seen him naked, and he didn't have a scratch on him. He'd come out whole physically, but emotionally...

"Thank you for your service."

He flipped us, so I was on my back, and he loomed over. I could barely see his face, but he reached up and stroked my hair back with his big palm. "You're thanking me? For what, doing my job or... " He rolled his hips, his very hard dick sliding up my inner thigh. "Or servicing you with this?"

I giggled, pleased to see I'd been able to pull him out of his dream. I knew some things about him—that he was a Green Beret and career military. He was the middle of the three Wolf brothers, but I didn't know much more than that. Even though I'd wanted to have a fling with him, there was more to him than just his hot bod and mad skills in the sack.

While it was obvious he wanted me, it seemed he was using his dick as deflection. I wanted it, definitely, but I wanted more from him, too. He was so dang big and strong, but he'd unintentionally let me see a vulnerable side. Something I doubted he let anyone know about.

"How long have you been in the military?"

His mouth dropped to my neck, and he kissed

and nibbled there. Angling my head, I gave him more room.

"Since I was eighteen," he murmured. He was a multi-tasker, answering my questions and making me hot.

"Career military then." It was hard to concentrate when he was licking and sucking at that spot where my neck and shoulder met.

"I'm on leave for a week. I head back to North Carolina right away."

I ran my hands through his short hair as he moved down to my collarbone. "Yet the nightmares follow wherever you go."

He paused, hovered over my nipple, then lifted his head. "I'm sure you've got shit that doesn't go away. Everyone does."

I licked my lips, nodded. I thought of my life. I had nothing to complain about. Sure, my parents were a hot mess and divorced, but whose weren't? My dad had been pretty much a no-show my whole life but paid for my college, which was a blessing. Although, per the bursar, he'd somehow forgotten for the fall. To him, money took the place of any kind of relationship. It was easy. Write a check twice a year and forget about me.

The only good thing about the guy was that he

gave me a half-sister. Amazingly, I'd found out Audrey existed through a mail-in DNA test. Once I contacted her, we'd become fast friends, even though she was nine years older. She was eager to have me as her only bridesmaid. Knowing about my baking hobby, she'd even asked me to make her wedding cake.

Right this second, I was in bed with a gorgeous, generous man.

Yet I had issues. Who didn't?

"You're right."

"What wakes you up at night, little girl?" he asked.

Absently, I stroked his close-cropped hair as I thought.

"Not being enough," I said. The words came surprisingly easy. Maybe it was because we were in the dark, in a motel room in the middle of nowhere that I admitted that. That this night was a bubble, a cocoon from the real world. "You know how people have those dreams where they're in public, and they're naked? Or they're in school, and they forgot to study for the test?"

In the darkness, I saw Colton's lips curve up. "Sure."

"Well, mine are like that, only in every dream,

my dad is there, but he's giving all his attention to someone else. Like my best friend or some random kid. Or his girlfriend of the week. Someone he deemed better than me." I forced a laugh. "I know, wah wah. It's nothing compared to what you go through. It's not life or death. Good and evil."

"Pain is pain," Colton said softly, trailing his lips over my shoulder. "Comparisons mean nothing. So your dad's a dick?"

My laugh was genuine this time. "You could say that. Not abusive or mean, but I could never earn his attention, you know? My parents were divorced. My mom worked her ass off to raise and support me while he just did the bare minimum. I mean, he paid child-support, but he didn't come to my piano recitals or school functions or anything. We had biweekly visits that wouldn't have happened if my mom hadn't insisted on them and usually consisted of him taking his current girlfriend somewhere fun and me tagging along." I sighed. "Anyway. I'm too old to have daddy issues."

Those daddy issues had transferred into man insecurities, but I wasn't going to tell him that.

Colton growled. "Little girl, maybe you're just looking for affection in the wrong place."

I rolled my hips up and into him. "I'm naked and

beneath you. I think it's pretty obvious where I'm looking for affection right about now."

He stilled, and for a second, I thought I'd said something wrong.

But then he moved one hand on my knee to open it wide. He settled into the space he made, then slid his fingers up the sensitive skin on the inside of my thigh to even *more* sensitive places.

"Gonna get you to scream my name again," he said as two fingers slipped inside, found my G-spot with an accuracy that should have been frightening.

My eyes fell closed, and I let go. Colton wasn't taking from me, he was giving. Not only was he generous with his orgasms, but he listened, focused on me. The last thought I had before his crazy skills shut my brain off was that he might have been right because, right now, Colton was giving me everything I'd been missing.

And wasn't that as scary as could be?

MARINA

. . .

I woke to the sound of water running. Not rain, but a shower. I blinked, looked around. Oh shit!

I'd forgotten where I was.

I sat up. Okay, no need to panic. I was just in a motel room with Audrey's brother-in-law, who didn't know who I was. I should tell him as soon as he got out.

How would that conversation go? *Hey, Colton, guess what? We're actually heading to the same place. Surprise!*

Would it be a good surprise or a bad surprise? Definitely bad. He was on leave, probably happy to fuck a willing woman. That was what sailors did on shore leave, right?

Butterflies took wing in my belly. I didn't think Colton was a guy who liked surprises. And to him, would it be a surprise or deception? He'd spanked my ass for fun, but what kind of punishment would he give me for tricking him, especially since he only signed up for one night? I licked my lips. He might not even punish me. He could reject me outright. For some reason, the idea of Colton hating me hit harder than expected.

Sheesh. Was it because I'd slept with him? He'd rocked my world last night—and again at around three a.m.—but one night, and I got attached?

That was stupid. I'd been looking for a fling. I'd gotten it. He'd fucked a stranger.

My pussy ached from all the attention it got. It didn't matter if he wanted to continue said fling for the rest of the week or not. I'd gotten what I needed. Insane man-made orgasms. Why, then, did the idea of him not wanting to see me again sink like a concrete block in the pit of my stomach?

I climbed out of bed. Actually, maybe it would be better to just bail because it was safer that way. Leave him before he left me. I'd have a few hours to get over it. Over him.

When Colton saw me at the ranch, he'd slap me on the ass and thank me for a good time. I just didn't want to hear it right now.

Yeah, maybe I was chickening out, but I had zero experience with one-night stands and what happened the morning after. Especially when he found out I'd known who he was all along and had taken advantage of that. Most guys wouldn't care about being *used* for their dick, but Colton wasn't just a guy. He was Audrey's future brother-in-law who I'd see off and on for the rest of my life.

I found my clothes laid out on the radiator where he must've put them to dry last night.

That little kindness made my chest ache. Colton

was perfect. Running felt cowardly. I wasn't really running—it was a safety check. He'd see me in a couple hours at the ranch, and I had to be A-OK by then.

I pulled on my shirt and leggings, grabbed my suitcase and slipped out the motel door, hoping I wasn't making a huge mistake.

See you, soon, cowboy.

COLTON

I SMILED when I heard movement in the motel room. My little mate was awake. I'd woken at my usual five for PT, my body so attuned to the daily regimen it was impossible to break. Even in a different time zone. But I didn't get up and run the usual five miles. Fuck, no. I'd lain awake beside her until the sun rose before getting up, afraid I'd wake her. But she'd slept deeply last night. Peacefully. I knew, because I dozed lightly most of the night, so my wolf could watch over her and because it was hard to sleep with a hard dick, even after taking her twice.

My wolf needed to know she wasn't going

anywhere. That no one would hurt her. That she was here in my arms. For the first time in... forever, I was calm. No restlessness. No panic at not finding *her*.

Some of that over-protectiveness would ease after I claimed and marked her, but I didn't care if it didn't. Protecting my mate was a goddamn honor. If it meant a thousand sleepless nights, I'd sign up in a heartbeat. Hell, there was no signing up. I was on the job.

I finished the shower and toweled off, pausing when I heard the click of the front door. My shifter hearing was strong enough to hear over the bathroom fan. She was probably getting something out of her car.

Still, that underlying anxiety that had kept me awake all night made me throw open the bathroom door to get eyes on her.

And I did.

Fucking driving away.

Aw, fuck no. No, no, no.

Dropping the towel, I yanked on my clothes, grabbed my shit and ran for the truck, but her car was already out of sight.

Goddammit. My mate just left, and I didn't even know her fucking name!

I took a breath, let it out. The morning air was

cool, the rain had cleared away for a bluebird sky and a soft breeze. Inside me, the storm was still raging.

No, it was okay. I knew which direction she headed. I could catch up to her. Tossing my stuff onto the passenger seat, I climbed in and started the engine.

I would find her. When I did, I would *not* let out the steamball of aggression my wolf was throwing around. I would not scare her or come on too strong. Her ass would get spanked pink.

Before I could do that, I needed to goddamn find her.

I returned to the place we met last night—where the road had washed out from the swollen creek. The raised water was gone now, and I drove right past. The pillar she'd stood on caught my eye, making something cinch in my chest. My mate was out there. Alone. Not with me.

I'd find her. I had to find her.

5

Marina

I PULLED up to the ranch house and tumbled out of the rental car, looking like a rumpled mess in yesterday's clothes. I knew Audrey and Boyd had their own little cabin somewhere on the property—Audrey'd told me all about the work they were starting on it—but I didn't know where. Based on the length of the driveway, Wolf Ranch was huge, so I parked in the main circle drive, in front of the house, figuring I could get directions.

The screen door banged open, and my dark-haired half-sister came flying out to greet me. "You finally made it!" She pulled me into a warm hug. "Getting caught in the storm last night must've been so stressful!"

I hadn't seen Audrey since Christmas when we'd had a week together. It had been too long, especially since she'd found a guy to marry since then.

"Actually, it worked out okay," I laughed, my chin over her shoulder where our bodies were still tangled together. She was all soft, gorgeous curves where I was flat and boy-like in comparison.

I only found out about the existence of Audrey a year ago, but we'd formed an instant bond. We looked nothing alike, but no one was going to tell me we weren't sisters. Not when the DNA test kit said so. It felt like I'd known her forever, and at the same time, as if we'd missed out on so much.

We'd both grown up as only children. She'd been raised by a single mom, my dad having pretty much been a sperm donor in her life. I used to dream of having a sibling, someone to share everything with. I'd honestly felt my whole childhood like someone was lacking, but I'd assumed it was my absentee dad. I didn't know the person I was really missing was Audrey.

When I'd learned that I had a half-sister in Chicago, I'd celebrated before I even called her. I'd just known we'd be besties, and we were. We didn't see each other often, me being in school in LA and her working as a doctor in Montana. Still, we talked all the time on the phone. And for me, just knowing she existed was awesome.

"Wait..." Audrey pulled away to peer in my face. "What do you mean it worked out okay?"

Heat crept up my neck, and I looked away, sure she'd be able to see I'd had crazy sex all night if she looked me in the eye.

"I'll tell you later," I said, seeing a giant Colton-lookalike looming behind Audrey.

She detached herself from me and squeezed my hand. "I'm just glad you're here. Marina, this is Boyd." Looking over her shoulder, I couldn't miss the way she beamed. Practically glowed as if she had an aura about her.

The big guy standing behind her looked just like his pics online. No, better. He was gorgeous, but his brother was hotter. Distracting myself from that train of thought, I threw myself at him, giving him just as warm a hug as I'd given Audrey. "Boyd! I'm so glad to meet you. I've heard *all* about you."

He let out a surprised laugh, probably at my over-exuberance, and wrapped one arm around my waist to squeeze me back. "Nice to meet you, too," he said as he fixed his cowboy hat. He paused, took a deep breath, then frowned. The way he stared at me made me blush, although I had no idea why. Finally, he said, "Let me get your suitcase, darlin'."

"Thanks, it's in the backseat. It wouldn't fit in the tiny trunk."

Audrey looped an arm through mine. "Come on in. You're going to stay here in the main house because Boyd and I only have one bedroom, which means only one bed."

"Right, and you're busy getting busy in that bed." I waggled my eyebrows, having heard about some of their sexy times.

"That's true." Audrey laughed. It was strange to see my serious older sister so at ease. She'd always been warm, but there was a light-heartedness about her now that hadn't been there before. I guessed that was what good sex with a hot rodeo champ would do for a woman. And love. I shouldn't discount that part. Audrey had been so sure Boyd was a player, but he'd proven her wrong and been ready for commitment.

She led me into the sprawling ranch house and up the stairs to my bedroom, which had the most incredible view of the mountains. Cream walls, stained wood trim, a brass bed with a handmade quilt that made the room quaint and... perfect.

Boyd stepped into the room and put my suitcase on what looked like an old hope chest. "I'll share your sister during the day, but at night, she's all mine." He grinned, completely unashamed.

Audrey rolled her eyes.

"Deal," I told him.

"I'll leave you two to catch up," he said. "I'll introduce you to Rob and the ranch hands when they come back from chores. Colton, who's taken leave from the army, should be here sometime soon, too. He and Rob will stay here in the house with you. The ranch hands sleep in the bunkhouse across the way."

"Your brothers, right?" I tried to ignore the pancake flip in my belly when I heard Colton's name. I already couldn't wait to see him again. What would he think when he got here and saw me?

Boyd nodded. "That's right. Colton texted and said he landed yesterday, but I haven't seen him. Maybe he got stuck in the same weather you did. He better get here soon because I'll kick his ass if he misses my wedding." Boyd shot Audrey a wink, and I was instantly in love. I meant, in love for her because he was damn charming and good looking to boot.

No wonder Audrey hadn't been sure if she could trust he was for real. He was almost too good to be true.

But then, again, so was his brother. In a more manly, bossy kind of way. More handsome, too, but I wasn't going to hurt this guy's ego by telling him that. Or that I knew Colton... biblically.

"Well, I'll go tackle a few chores," Boyd drawled, tossing another wink at his bride. So damn cute.

"Eek! I'm so excited for you guys," I squealed as he sauntered out. Audrey watched his backside as he did so. I did, too, because it was quite a show.

"Do you want to get refreshed? Shower? Change?" Audrey asked when he was finally out of sight.

"Actually, I would feel better if I got a jump start on baking the wedding cake. I'm totally behind since I didn't get here last night. I want to have time to decorate it, and sometimes that takes me a while because I'm not a pro."

"I don't know, from the pictures you've sent me, the birthday cakes you've made for your friends are as professional as they come."

I laughed. "That doesn't mean they don't take me twice as long as they should."

"You know we don't need anything, fancy, right? It's a barn wedding, after all."

"Seeing the groom and this place? It sounds perfect. No matter the setting, you should have the perfect cake," I insisted. "I just hope you have a fridge big enough to store it."

"The bunk house has an industrial sized one. I told the guys to make a space... and not to eat it."

"Problem solved." I held my hands in front of me like I was praying. "Please just let me go crazy. I've always wanted to bake a wedding cake. You're making my dreams come true here."

"Well, I am the beneficiary of those dreams, so it works for me. Come on, I'll show you to the kitchen." She pushed her glasses up her nose. "It's huge—you'll love it."

I couldn't help but feel excited about working on Audrey's cake... in a kitchen that sounded incredible. "Let me grab my recipe."

I pulled it from my purse then followed Audrey back down the back stairs that led right into... yup, the fabulous kitchen. It wasn't flashy—no contemporary granite or stainless steel. I knew the Wolf parents had been killed in a car accident when Boyd was only twelve. I doubted Rob, the brother who lived in the house full time, had done any updates since then. It didn't matter. It was rustic and perfect, with a huge farm table that would be ideal for frosting and assembling the cake. I envisioned three square tiers with white buttercream frosting and piped flowers that matched what was to be in Audrey's bouquet.

"I emailed my dad that I was coming here for the wedding," I said, hoping the news wouldn't drop like a bomb. I winced a little when she turned round eyes on me. "I'm sorry. Was that okay? I'm sorry, not *my* dad. He's your dad, too."

She shook her head. "He is *your* dad. I've only met him once. He hasn't made any overtures to connect, so..."

She didn't need to say more, only leaned a hip against the counter.

"I understand." I did. I felt an emptiness where I should have felt love for my father. Disappointment. "I grew up with him, and he doesn't try to connect with me. Or, it seems, to pay the school bill," I muttered the last to myself. "You'd think he'd be interested that I was here with you. Whatever."

She just offered a shrug, clearly beyond the point of caring about a dad who'd been MIA her entire life.

"Anyway," I replied with a sigh. "He didn't

respond. Go figure." I said the last on a whisper and glanced at her through my lashes.

He was too busy in his own life to notice what was going on in his daughters' lives. Like a wedding. I tried. I'd always tried to connect with him. I was just now coming to realize it was wasted hope. Especially after meeting Audrey because he had a child, a real person, who he should have wanted to connect with but didn't.

Audrey's face turned a little pink—whether it was from anger or disappointment, I couldn't be sure. "It doesn't matter. Really. I never knew him. It sounds like you've got more issues with him than I do." She went to a lower cabinet and pulled out some mixing bowls.

She kept busy finding measuring cups and sifters and ingredients. It took her a little while to search, and I remembered this wasn't her kitchen. She'd never lived in this house.

I licked my lips and stood out of her way as she set everything on the counter. "Yeah, and see where that's gotten me."

"It's gotten you here to bake me a wedding cake." She turned her head from the open fridge and smiled. "If you want to go into baking for a career, do it."

"I'm good at engineering," I said, as if pleading my case for spending three years in a major I hated.

"Of course, you are. You're super smart. But do you love it?"

I pursed my lips and shrugged, not ready to admit anything.

"Don't bowl me over with your enthusiasm," she countered, holding the container of eggs. "Here. I'm not sure what else you need. I get my cakes at the store, so I'm not going to be any help."

"You deliver babies. You don't have to be able to bake."

She gave a little huff of laughter. "You'd think *because* I can deliver babies, I could make a cake. But, no." She tucked her long hair back behind her ear. In jeans and a cute t-shirt, she looked more cowgirl than doctor. She had the arm candy, so all that was missing was the boots.

I pulled out a chair at the table. "Sit here and talk while I work."

Happily, she sat down, then popped back up. "Coffee."

I went over to the double oven to turn it on as she went over to the coffeemaker and poured herself a cup.

"Give me all the details of the wedding," I said as

I got to work. She hadn't pulled out a stand mixer—she probably didn't even know what one was—so I found it on a shelf in the walk-in pantry.

I listened to her tell about how it was going to be a small event, about twenty people. She'd invited a few girlfriends she worked with. I learned the Wolf family was only the three brothers, but there were about ten who lived and worked on the ranch plus other close friends who lived up in the hills who were also invited.

A few guys who called themselves the Barn Cats volunteered to play their bluegrass instruments. Fairy lights were being strung from the open barn doors, and a simple lunch was being catered by someone in town.

To me, it sounded perfect. I didn't want a big event when I got married, not interested in being the center of attention. I was more eager for a guy than for the wedding.

That made me think of Colton. My pussy had gotten a workout, not once, but twice. I was tired, too, although I had no regrets about our three in the morning sexy times.

I turned and hit the coffee pot myself, grabbing a mug off the stand that was right beside it. Colton hadn't shown up. Obviously. I started to wonder what I was going to do when he did. If he'd see me and pretend we didn't know each other. Would he be mad?

I dropped into the mixer the amount of butter for the three layers and turned it on to cream. The noise of the machine didn't allow for much talking, so I measured out the sugar and added it, letting my mind wander back to Colton. My quick and not-pleasant introduction to sex back in high school had left me wanting and lacking in skill.

That had been resolved last night. I had an inner seductress in me, and I realized I didn't want to put her back. But it was Colton my pussy craved. His bossiness, his dominance. God, even the slap of his hand on my bare ass.

I just had no idea if he wanted more or not because when I'd left him in that motel room, I'd missed my chance for answers. The idea of getting the wrong answer left me too vulnerable. Exposed. The love'-em-and-leave-'em guy from college had validated how unexciting I was. It was best to shrug Colton Wolf off as no more than a wild night.

A night I'd be reliving with my vibrator for the rest of my life.

Besides, it was safer this way. I had a life back in LA. Plans. He had a life. Commitments. Guns and war and tactical maneuvers. Army stuff that was way more important than a one-night-stand in Montana motel room.

We could never be more than a fling. A fling that had flung.

I did not under any circumstances need him to want me...

Who was I kidding? That's exactly what I wanted. Big time.

6

Colton

I DROVE through every small town between the motel and Wolf Ranch looking for her car. Fortunately, the towns were small, so it was easy to canvas the streets before moving on. Unfortunately, I hadn't found her. I had no choice but to go to the ranch. For now.

I hadn't been back in almost two years, and as I pulled up in front of the main house, I noticed what had changed. Not fucking much. The house had a fresh coat of paint. White flowers instead of red were in the beds below the porch. In the distance, I saw the fencing around the corral had been replaced.

I climbed from the truck, slung my bag over my shoulder. It felt good to be home, to be standing on the hard-packed ground I knew so well. The sense of belonging, the familiarity was in my DNA. My wolf was happy to be here... although he was a grumpy fuck for not knowing where our mate was.

So was I. Once my approval for leave had gone through—my stint was almost up, and I had to decide if I wanted to re-up, but that was to figure out later—all I'd thought about was getting back here, dumping my shit, shifting, then running. Now, I'd roam, but it would be to search all over this part of Montana to find my fucking mate. And not in wolf form.

Dammit.

Before last night, I'd had no idea who she was or where she was. Now, I still didn't know, but I knew she existed. That our connection was perfect. Sweet.

Wild.

The agony was so much worse now. My wolf and the moon madness pushed at me. Swearing, I stomped up the steps and through the front door. When I was a kid, the scent of pot roast would greet me along with our old dog, Charlie. My mom would be in the kitchen, Boyd often at the kitchen table forced to do homework or eating a snack. Rob would be off with my dad doing... alpha shit. Now, it wasn't the scent of Crockpot meat that hit me but baked goods and something sweet. My wolf sat up and took notice. My dick picked up on it too and got instantly hard, which made no fucking sense.

As I adjusted myself, Boyd came down the hall. "You never could stop playing with your dick."

The grin on his face accompanied his mocking tone.

He hugged me hard, slapping my back. For being my little brother, he had an inch on me. I could still take him on in a fist fight, but I'd rather face a hidden sniper than climb on the back of a bull, like he used to do every day.

"Hey, brother." I slapped him right back. I couldn't help but grin at him. Fuck, he looked good. That underlying rebellion and anger he always had simmering had faded, was replaced by an aura of contentedness. "And I heard you don't have to tug on yours all alone anymore."

He stepped back, winked. "Damn straight."

"You turning into Betty Crocker now?" I asked,

taking another sniff of the air. I could swear I smelled my mate. Her scent must've carried on my clothes. I remembered her taste on my tongue, but this was different. Visceral.

"Nah, the women are making the wedding cake. They've been in there for two hours, and it smells damned good."

The moon madness was definitely fucking with me if I was confusing my mate with baked goods.

"Women? I thought you found one mate, not two."

He tipped his hat back. Fuck, he looked happy. Potent jealousy shot through me, but I instantly pushed it down. He wasn't the only Wolf brother to find his mate. He *was* the only one who knew where his fucking mate was, though. I might've been older and wiser, but who was the dumbass now?

Me.

"Marina's making it," he said, and I'd forgotten what he was talking about. Oh yeah, cake. "Audrey's watching. She might have gone to medical school for four years, but she can barely boil water."

"Who's Marina?"

"Her little sister—half-sister, actually—from LA."

He sniffed, then his eyes widened.

"What?" I asked.

A slow smile spread across his face. "Nothing. Nothing at all."

I was going to ask him what the fuck he was not telling me, but Rob's voice cut me off. "Hey—I expected you to parachute in or something."

I turned as he came up the porch steps. Behind him were two of our ranch hands and pack members, Levi and Clint.

The trio were fucking huge. They didn't have to do morning calisthenics and ten mile runs with fully loaded packs to be sturdy fuckers. They also had all the room to shift and run.

Shit, I hadn't realized how much I missed being home.

"The airlines don't like me opening the emergency exit," I countered as Rob stepped close. "Dude, is that gray hair?"

Rob touched the side of his head and rolled his eyes. "Fucker."

"It's good to see you." It was. My fellow soldiers were brothers not of blood, but Rob and Boyd... the other shifters on the ranch, the connection went deep. They knew the truth, knew the real me. *All* of me.

"Expected you last night," Rob said, slapping me

on the shoulder, which was him showing affection. He wasn't much of a hugger.

The screen door banged behind Levi. I shook his hand and Clint's.

"The storm flooded a creek on county road ninety-three. Had to spend the night in Tremont."

Boyd looked me over. This morning, I'd tossed on the same clothes as the day before in my rush to go after my mate. "What did you do, sleep in your truck? You look like you barely slept."

My wolf preened at our prowess, then whined because we'd lost her. *Her.* What the fuck was her name? Why did I not make it my number one priority to know every detail about her? I'd gotten cocky, thinking I had her. Thinking I'd take it slow and not scare her off. And then she fucking *left*. *Where* the fuck was she?

"Yeah, found some trouble."

In the form of a five-foot-two she-devil who soothed my wolf, emptied my balls and sated my dick. Then bolted like a pissed off bull out of a chute.

Boyd smirked.

"Problem?" Rob asked, one brow raised. He was alpha now, but he'd come into the role when he was only eighteen. Still, he had it down, barely showing any emotion below his signature gruffness.

"Nothing I can't handle." I'd find her and light her ass up for leaving me. Then I'd fuck her and maybe that ass, reminding her who was in fucking charge. It wasn't her.

"We were thinking you liked a big sandbox instead of home," Levi commented.

I thought of the tour I'd finished in Afghanistan. The desert climate did shit for me. I couldn't shift and run. Hot as fuck, especially under fur.

"Had to keep my fellow soldiers safe," I replied. It was true. I had better hearing, eyesight, sense of smell. I couldn't die very easily. All of that was why I'd climbed quickly through the ranks, but it didn't always keep my soldiers alive. And lately, with the fucking moon madness, I had to question my own abilities on the job. I didn't want to be a danger to my team, and I felt I was more of a liability than an asset these days.

"You're getting fucking old. Maybe it's time to let someone else save the world?" Levi continued.

I thought of my men and at first was pissed Levi thought I'd abandon them, but he was right. It was my job to lead them, regardless of our orders. But when I hit thirty, I'd become restless for more. My wolf let me know it was time to focus on finding a mate and claiming her. He wanted to protect a mate. Pups.

I wasn't at retirement age yet, but maybe it was time for someone else to save the world, just as Levi said. No one else on base had a wolf inside them.

"Maybe," I replied, not ready to tell him I was thinking the same thing. It was time to decide to re-up, but it seemed my wolf had made the decision for me. Same went for the woman from last night. My fucking mystery mate.

"Why the fuck are we standing here? Time you met my woman," Boyd said, then turned to lead us all toward the kitchen.

The scent of vanilla and sugary cake got stronger as we cut down the hallway to the back of the house. Mom had wanted a huge kitchen, and Dad had given her one. A big central counter, huge rustic farm table and chairs to seat the five of us along with the shifters living at the ranch. It even had a fireplace for the cold Montana winters.

Mom and Dad had been gone now over fifteen years, so it'd been a while since I'd smelled scents like these in the house. Not that Rob didn't cook, but he didn't fucking bake.

"Darlin', Colton finally got here."

Boyd went over to a woman and dropped a kiss

on her lips. I didn't know if she had blonde hair or two heads or had fairy wings because all I saw was the other woman standing at the counter with a metal spatula in her hand.

Her.

My mate's scent hit me now. Clearly, it had been masked by the baked goods on the counter and in the oven, but no wonder I'd gotten hard when I'd come in the front door. She'd been here frosting a fucking cake while I'd been roaming the streets for her.

"Are you fucking kidding me?" I growled.

Everyone froze and stared.

"Hi," she said, her voice a breathy whisper. My wolf howled. My hands clenched. It was a good thing the counter was between us.

"Ha, I knew it," Boyd said on a laugh.

"How the fuck did you know?" I asked him.

He sniffed the air.

I raised my hand to shut him up, in case he felt like sticking his damned nose... literally none of his fucking business. I didn't look his way, didn't break eye contact with her. Marina.

My mate was Audrey's little fucking sister. Which meant...

"You knew who I was," I said to her.

I was beyond pissed.

She nodded and bit her lip. She had on the same clothes as the night before, just like me. Her hair was up in a bun, and her cheeks flushed from the heat in the kitchen. She looked perfect. Whole. *Here.*

And yet I was so angry at her.

"Surprise!" She faked a smile and raised her shoulders in a funny shrug.

"Um, you two know each other?" Rob asked from behind me.

"She's my fucking ma—," I stopped because I didn't know if Marina even knew what we were. Audrey did, but it was against pack law to reveal to humans. The existence of shifters was a closely-guarded secret. Audrey knew since my brother fucking bit her neck and claimed her. Marina would need to know before I claimed her as well, but Boyd and Audrey shouldn't have told her. "She's my fucking..."

Boyd laughed and exchanged an incredulous glance at Rob. "Wow."

"Your what?" Marina demanded, hands on hips.

"Why didn't you tell me who you were, little girl?" I tried to change the subject.

She lifted her chin. "I wasn't sure if you had some rule against screwing little sisters."

"Uh—" Rob began.

Audrey gasped.

Marina blushed. "I thought a one-night stand would sit better with you."

"You think I usually fuck strangers in motel rooms?" I snarled, even though she had no idea why I actually brought her there.

"I'm sure you've done something like that before," she countered.

"You knew who I was." It dawned on me that she really had been the one doing the seducing. She might have been young and inexperienced, but she'd known what she was doing last night. Part of me was relieved that she wouldn't have slept with a stranger, the other part was furious at being used.

For sex.

By my own mate.

My very *human* who didn't know she was my mate.

"Guys—" Rob tried to cut in.

"You slept with me without even knowing my name," she added.

"You slept with Colton?" Audrey asked, but neither of us looked her way.

"I told you last night it wasn't necessary," I said to Marina.

Crossing her arms over her chest, she added, "Total one-night stand move."

"It's not just one night. You're—"

"Guys!" Rob said, stepping around the counter, so he stood between us. "She's the trouble you ran into last night?"

Marina sputtered. "I'm *trouble?*"

"Little girl, you're nothing but. Let me explain all the ways." I stalked around the counter toward her, and Rob smartly moved out of my way. I didn't slow, only bent down and tossed her over my shoulder. It felt good to have her in my arms. Fuck, did she push my buttons. But I was relieved to know where she was, that she was safe. Whole.

Now that I did, I could take care of her. Smack her cute ass for putting me through that shit. Satisfy her. And soon, I would tell her she's my mate. Explain it all.

It would be easier for her to swallow than I feared last night, since her sister had already been marked and brought into the pack.

As I left the kitchen and went up the back stairs, I called out, "I'm stealing your little sister, Audrey. I'll take good care of her, though. I promise. Take care of that cake, will you?"

I heard smothered laughter from the group.

"You upset my future little sister, I'm gonna have to kill you!" Boyd called after me, but there was a chortle in his voice, too.

7

Marina

"Colton!" I kicked my legs as my giant sexy Green Beret carried me up the stairs and down a hall. "What are you doing?"

"You thought I'd have a problem with screwing little sisters, huh?" A heavy palm fell on my ass, and I squealed.

"Ow!"

"Little girl, I'm gonna smack that ass until it's rosy. Last night was *not* a one-night stand for me. And I did *not* appreciate you running off."

My heartbeat kicked up in speed, but I wasn't

afraid. I never expected this level of reaction from him, and frankly, it thrilled me. I'd made it easy for him. Gave him an out. I'd thought it might be a little awkward when he found me here. Thought we'd keep it our secret, and he might chew me out in private later for tricking him into sex with a person he thought was a stranger. With a person who he might consider too young for him. Or off-limits.

But this? This was freaking exciting. He hadn't been ashamed about what we'd done. He'd admitted it in front of everyone. Very loudly. Very clearly. Now he wanted me alone in, I assumed, his room. I was in dangerous territory here because he was only here for a week. He might want more from me sexually, but he'd be gone before the leftover wedding cake was even finished.

He kicked open a door, stepped in and shut it behind us. The second he dropped my feet to the floor, he tugged my t-shirt off over my head. My nipples pebbled up, eager for his attention.

Mmm. Yes, please. I'd take more of Colton Wolf's attention any day.

I looked around. Definitely his bedroom. The walls were tan but had posters on them. A shelf over a desk in the corner had trophies.

He sat on his bed and pulled me between his

knees, his hands stroking up and down my hips, squeezing my ass. It was like he couldn't get enough of me, an intoxicating feeling. Since I never wore a bra, I was bare from the waist up. My nipples were hard from being exposed to the cool air. Who was I kidding? They got hard over his caveman behavior.

"S-so you don't have a problem with screwing little sisters?" My voice came out breathless and small.

"Not this little sister." His words came out as a dark rumble as his gaze roved over me, honing in on my breasts. "But you are in so much trouble with me, little girl."

He took a deep breath, his nostrils flaring. I remembered this action from the night before, as if he were trying to breathe me in. A thrill of excitement shot up my spine, and my panties grew damp.

"So you said," I purred, feigning more confidence than I had. But he had enough confidence and experience for the both of us. Who marched in, threw a girl he only had sex with once—make that twice—over his shoulder and carried her to his room?

I guessed he knew I was receptive.

And he was possessive. I loved that.

He hooked his thumbs in my yoga pants and dragged them down my thighs. Wow. Okay, I guessed we were doing this. He wasted no time in getting right to it. I kicked off my shoes, so I could step out of the pants. I was in nothing but my G-string, and Colton growled like a wild animal, stroking his hands up and down my legs like he couldn't get enough of me.

But then he pulled my torso down over one thigh and onto the bed and gave my ass three hard spanks. I bucked.

"Eek! Ow! Oh my God!" I wriggled, a little scared, a little offended. A lot turned on.

"That's not going to work." He was already rubbing away the sting, his big palm squeezing and massaging my smarting cheeks. "That's gonna be way too loud, isn't it, little girl? *Marina,*" he added, like he wanted to get used to saying my name. "We wouldn't want the whole ranch to hear you get your spanking."

Oh Jesus. Why did that make my belly flip and fresh arousal seep between my legs?

He kept me in that position, though, squeezing and massaging my ass, rubbing his fingers through my wetness. "I have to admit, I'm glad you knew who I was."

"I'm glad you don't have a problem with little sisters."

His hand circling my ass went still. "Exactly how *little* are we talking?" He sounded slightly choked.

Oh crap. I didn't want this to stop. Would he think twenty-one was too young? He had to be ten years older than I was.

"I'm legal, if that's what you're worried about," I said tartly.

He gave me two more spanks that made me squeal. "I asked you a question, sweetness." He massaged my ass again, and my core turned molten. "I expect an answer."

"Twenty-one."

"Twenty-one," he repeated, and I swore I heard disappointment in his tone. "And still in college. How many years left?"

"One."

"Fuck," he muttered and lifted me from his thigh.

"What?" I sat on his opposite knee and eyed him, suddenly feeling exposed. I was completely naked, and he had all his clothes on. And he'd stopped our fun time. Was he changing his mind about having sex now? "It's not like you're that old."

Please, no. Don't shut this down. I needed this. My body needed this. My spirit needed this.

He shook his head, cupping my breast. I bit my lip and rocked on his lap to keep from moaning wantonly. He already had me burning everywhere for him. "Older than you. Not just in years, but in life. The shit I've seen... " He sounded like he was convincing himself.

I thought of the nightmare he had the night before, knew he'd been deployed. He was right, I'd barely lived in comparison. So while I was riled, I couldn't be mad at him for serving our country while I was in elementary school. "I know you're going back to your base. You've made that very clear."

"And you're going back to college. You're young. It's all right. I can work with it."

Ha. I knew I had been right to keep my identity a secret last night. He *did* have qualms but was eager for more as much as me.

I moved to straddle him, ready to move this thing forward, but his lips tipped up, and he gripped my waist. "Uh uh. You are not in charge here, Marina. And I believe punishment is still in order."

Lordy. Every time he said *punishment* my pussy clenched. "What's my punishment?" I sounded out of breath.

"Hmm." He lifted me off his knee and followed me to stand. "Spanking's too loud. I think you might need to be tied up and eaten."

Everything clenched. Pussy. Anus. Diaphragm. *Yes, please, Mr. Wolf.*

"Oh my God. I'm going to be eaten by the big, bad Wolf."

Colton smirked. "You have no idea, little girl." He picked me up by the waist like dead-lifting a hundred and ten pounds was a total cinch and tossed me on my back on the bed. I sat up and scooted back, a nervous laugh escaping my lips as he loomed over me, then grabbed my ankles and tugged them wide. "Don't move. You stay right where I put you." He walked to the dresser and pulled open a drawer. "Hmm. What will I tie you with?" He shut the top drawer and opened the next one, using one hand to scoot things around as he peered in. "Uh huh." He pulled out a wrinkled navy blue tie and tossed it on the bed. Then a red one. Then silver.

Were they his? "It's hard to picture you in a tie," I confessed, watching his every move. Even though he wore the same clothes as the night before, he was gorgeous. Rumpled looked damned good on him. I could imagine him in uniform, and that would probably ruin me.

He picked one up and snapped it between two hands, like it was a threat. "Yeah, that's why they're in my dresser," he said. "I think some asshole gave them to me for graduation. Since I enlisted a week later, they're still sitting here."

He got busy tying my right ankle to the leg of the bed, then the left. "I'll have to be sure to send a thank you note. Who knew they'd be put to such... good use?"

Being so exposed—spread wide for him and tied down did crazy things to my body. I trembled visibly, my inner thighs shaking, my belly shuddering in with each breath. Colton dropped a hand on my ankle and stroked slowly up. "You okay, sweetness? Are you scared?"

I shook my head.

"Excited, then." His gaze was on my pussy where he could see the truth. I was wet. No one had gotten me like this before, my eagerness coating even my thighs.

My heart pounded as I nodded. I couldn't lie.

"Use your words, sweetness." He knelt between my legs, set his big palms on my inner thighs and took a long swipe of his tongue between my legs.

I warbled out an answering cry, my hips bucking.

"You could say, *Yes, sir.* Or even, *Yes, Daddy.*" He winked up at me from my pussy.

I picked up the pillow by my head and hurled it

at him, giggling. "I'm not calling you, *Daddy*. The last thing I want to do is think of my dad when I'm with you."

"*Sir* will do, then." He grinned back. "Especially when you're tied up and at my mercy." He knelt up, looped the fill-in rope around my throat, the crisscross in the back. He tied each of my wrists with an end.

I tested his work. If I moved my arms, it tightened the slack around my neck. A thrill shot through me. Wild. Intense.

"I don't think this is the knot work the Boys Scouts had in mind," I replied, my tone sarcastic. The idea, though, that I wasn't actually tied down but couldn't do anything with my hands sent a shiver through me. I had to keep my palms against my neck, or I'd tighten the tie myself.

Oh. My. God. I'd never been tied up before, never knew it was even hot. He didn't need to pin me down to keep me in place.

He grinned. "Maybe I should take a picture and send it to the Scoutmaster."

Pulling his cell from his back pocket of his cargo pants, I stilled. "You wouldn't."

"I think you tied up and at my mercy might give Mr. O'Roarke a heart attack." He lifted his cell and aimed it at me, then winked. "This one's just for me to remember how naughty my little girl can be."

I licked my lips and realized he hadn't taken the picture. He was waiting for me. I was naked, spread eagle and tied up. At his mercy. He was clothed, but far from unaffected. I couldn't miss the way his dick tented the front of his pants. He was as into this as I was.

I nodded, then remembered what he said. "Yes, sir."

Heat flared in his eyes, and he took a picture. "Fucking gorgeous."

I whimpered, trying to imagine what I looked like to him.

Tossing the cell onto the bed, he said, "I want to hear, *I'm sorry I bailed on you this morning, sir.*"

I had to wonder if he was ever going to let me up. This was punishment, definitely. I couldn't touch myself, and he wasn't touching me. He'd only licked me once, and I was dying. Aching. Clenching with the need to get off.

"Little girl," he warned. He took a nipple between his thumb and forefinger. Tugged gently, then pinched. I arched my back and moaned, which had him letting go.

"You want to come?"

I nodded, my hair sliding over the bed behind me.

"Do you decide how and when you come?" he all but growled. He tweaked my other nipple, this time with a little more pressure. My hands jerked, and it tugged about my neck.

I was literally one bean-flick away from an orgasm. I didn't know why I trusted this guy who I hardly knew to do these depraved things to me, but I did. And his bossy, controlling manner just readied me to hurtle over the edge into bliss. I arched, pushing my small breasts toward the ceiling silently begging for him to play with them some more. My legs shook with sexual tension. "I-I'm sorry I bailed on you this morning, sir. But I'm not sorry I didn't tell you who I was last night because it was a really satisfying hookup."

Colton's brows slammed down, and he looked pissed. "Hook-up? I am not your hook-up, little girl." He gave my pussy a light slap, then brought his fingers to his mouth, licked my arousal from them.

I dragged my lower lip through my teeth and mewled at the wicked pain/pleasure. "Wh-what are you, then?"

He glowered for a moment, but it was like he couldn't figure out what to say. "I'm the guy who's about to torture your sweet little body, Marina. Your leaving made me out of control. Now it's your turn to know what it feels like. And you're gonna take it like a good girl."

My lashes fluttered as my eyes rolled back in my head.

"I know. Just for fun. Just for now. I thought last night was a one-off, but... okay. I'll take a little more dick."

"Dick? How about my mouth first?"

He dropped back down between my tied legs, parted me with his thumbs and trailed the tip of his tongue in a slow line around all my lady bits.

The trembling in my inner thighs increased. Even more heat flooded my lower region. The surface of my skin prickled everywhere, sensitized for his touch. He traced a tiny circle around my clit. I cried out, my thighs thrashing. I wanted to close them around his head, to kick out at the incredible sensations, but he'd tied me too well.

"Ohhhh," I moaned. "Please."

He lifted his head, his lips glossy with my juices. He traded his tongue for his thumb, rubbing lightly over my magic button. "Please let you come?"

I nodded vigorously. "Yes." It came out as more of a gasp than a word.

He switched and plunged his thumb into my pussy as he shook his head. "I don't think so." There was a wicked smirk on his face that cut through the haze of lust. He rubbed his palm over my clit as he plunged his thumb in and out, then lowered his head to use his tongue again.

"Wh-what?"

I don't know why I was talking. His tongue was where I needed it—I shouldn't interrupt him. He lifted his head and pulled his thumb out. "This is punishment, sweetness." He slapped my clit lightly with his fingertips, and I jerked. "I think I'll keep you on edge for hours."

"Oh!" It was all I could think to say. Dismay and lust simultaneously slammed through me and collided, leaving me stupid and panting.

Colton returned to licking and stroking while I grew more feverish.

"Colton," I started pleading. "I need... I need."

"Oh, I know what you need, little girl. You need to be taught a lesson."

"I'm sorry!" I exclaimed. And I really was. Of course, I would also say anything at that moment to get him to bring me to orgasm.

"You're sorry you ran away from me?" he

demanded, pushing my asscheeks open and rimming my anus.

I moaned. Loud. In the motel room, Colton had played with my ass with his finger. But this? It was soooo naughty. Especially because it felt so good. How did he know I liked all this stuff when I didn't even know myself?

He lifted his head again. "While I love hearing you get off, it's just for me. Not for everyone downstairs."

"Then stop doing that," I snapped.

He slapped my pussy again. "You want me to stop?" He shrugged, then sat up. "Okay, I'll stop. You can go back downstairs with hard nipples and a needy pussy."

"No." I tugged on my hands, which tugged on my throat. "No, don't stop."

"That's right. Because you need what only I can give you." He circled a finger around my entrance, coated it in my cream, then smeared it over my back entrance. "You like ass play, don't you, naughty girl?"

"With you," I whispered.

He groaned. "Then you'll get me. In there."

I squirmed, equally aroused and fearful of the idea. I'd seen his dick, knew how big it was. He was a tight fit in my pussy. "Now?"

The corner of his mouth turned up. "No lube. I didn't get around to ass fucking in my childhood bedroom."

I wasn't sure if I was disappointed or relieved.

"The way you're writhing on the bed, I'm not so sure if it would be a punishment, anyway."

"Colton," I breathed.

He grabbed my t-shirt off the floor. "Here. Put this in your mouth to quiet you down." Rolling it into a pseudo-twist, he set the center in front of my mouth. I looked up at him, at how he was so fucking patient, and opened. I bit down on it, my mouth wetting the fabric. I could spit it out, but he was right. I was loud with him, and while the house was big, my sister was downstairs. And Colton's brothers. And the ranch hands. I had no doubt they knew what we were up to, but I wasn't sure if I could face any of them if they'd heard me scream and beg and whimper Colton's name.

"Good girl. Now, where was I?" He looked me over, then settled back between my spread thighs. "Right. About. Here."

His hands cupped my butt, and he licked me from ass to clit and back again. He was exceptional at oral. So good that he got me to the brink of coming, then stopped. He nipped the inside of my thigh or blew on my swollen flesh. Then he got his fingers involved, and I was so strung out, so over the top with need to come that I was coated in sweat. My muscles quivered. My nipples were no longer hard, but soft, plump tips. My ass had a finger in it, nice and deep. He didn't do anything with it, just put it there, I thought, because he could.

And because I liked it. He was doing to me whatever he wanted, and I had to take it. I couldn't move. I could only feel, and it was so much. Too much.

Tears leaked down my temples, and I couldn't even cry out any more, only whimper. Propping up on one hand, he lifted the t-shift from my mouth. "This punishment, sweetheart? It's not just torturing you."

He sat back, undid his pants, pushed them down, so his dick sprung free. So large, so heavy. Today, it was darker, the veins up the length bulging, the crown almost bursting it was so swollen. Pre-cum dripped down the length as if it were a leaky faucet.

He grabbed a condom from his pocket, rolled it down his length. They had to be from the XXL box.

Reaching behind his head, he tugged off his shirt. He was so gorgeous. That body. That dick. I needed him.

"I'm going to get in you now, and you're going to

come. You've been waiting for my dick like a good girl."

Leaning forward he undid the tie around one of my wrists. "I'm going to fuck you good and hard, and I don't want you to choke. Grab the pillow. Yes, like that. Now don't let go."

I nodded, and he moved so his dick was right at my entrance. He didn't linger, only painted the tip in my cream, then thrust into me in one long stroke.

My sensitive tissues opened for him, the fit snug, but that made me feel every slick inch of him. I came, just as he'd said. He hadn't put his fingers inside my pussy, and it made me even greedier for all of him. Yet, my ass tingled because it was now empty.

I clenched as I came on a wail.

"Fuck," he growled as he began to do just as he'd said and fucked me into the bed.

I gasped as I came, the pleasure a relief. I had no idea how long he played and punished me, taunting me with this orgasm. But now, I'd never come like this before. My inner walls rippling, trying to pull him even deeper.

The bed slammed against the wall. Colton growled as he pounded into me, our flesh slapping. He'd been so attentive, so focused on every nuance of my body. Now, he was lost. He had no rhythm or cadence to the hard pounding, only driving himself to the pleasure he'd been missing out on as well.

I gripped the pillow and had to wonder if I'd rip it, if feathers would fly around us.

I needed everything he could give. Last night had been wild. This... carnal. He'd proven that I was at his mercy, that only he could make my body writhe and sweat, come like never before. I saw stars. When he rolled his hips and ground down on my clit, I came once more, this time almost painful in the bliss.

And yet, in less than a minute, he thrust deep and growled, his head tucking into my neck as he came. I felt it, hot and never ending, filling me. He hadn't spoken once he got inside me, except for one word.

Mine, he'd said. Over and over. And now, with his breathing ragged against my neck, he said it again. Our skin was slick and stuck together. My pussy was over-sensitive. His weight pinned me to his childhood bed. This time, when he said the word, it was with a snarl. "*Mine.*"

I believed him. I was ruined for all others. I could never be like this with anyone else. I couldn't let go as I had. I couldn't trust in such a way.

When I finally released the pillow and stroked over his heated back, his teeth grazed along my neck, his tongue licking at the skin there.

I thought he'd soften and pull out, but he didn't. Within a minute, he pushed up onto his hands, loomed over me and began to rock into me again.

"I'm not done with you, little one." With those words, he pulled out while holding the base of the condom, then sitting back on his heels, slipped it off, grabbed a tissue from the dresser and disposed of it. He grabbed another from his pants, put it on. How many did he carry on him?

"Again? Now?"

"Again. Now."

I moaned, not sure if I could die from too much good sex.

He moved his hips, slower now, more leisurely. "The scent of fucking... it's all over you."

"I don't think I can come again," I admitted.

"You can. You will."

And I did.

8

COLTON

I FUCKED my mate into exhaustion. Only when she was asleep in my bed, naked and marked with my scent, did I leave her. I showered, dressed in fresh clothes, then shut the door behind her to track down my brothers.

She may have been muffled with her t-shirt, but Marina couldn't be quiet if she tried. That made my wolf howl because a mate shouldn't have to be quiet while getting eaten out. She should scream her pleasure. Anytime. All the time.

Everyone on the ranch but Audrey was a shifter, and we had incredible hearing. They may not have heard Marina, but they definitely heard me. I didn't hold back once I'd gotten inside her. I couldn't have even if someone held a gun to my head. I'd probably have to fix the drywall later, but it had been worth it. No male shifter who'd heard us would seek her attention. Marina was mine. My scent was all over her.

The second time I fucked her, I'd pulled the condom off and spilled all over her breasts and belly to mark her as mine. I couldn't bite her and claim her yet as I wanted. Fuck, did I want to sink my teeth into her sweet flesh. My wolf was pissed I hadn't yet. Didn't understand why I was waiting because we were so close to the full moon. The scent of her, the taste of her had my teeth elongating to do just that. I hadn't spent over a decade in the military without an iron will. I'd had to use it with Marina.

She might've surprised the fuck out of me downstairs, but I had a bigger fucking surprise in store for her. Before I mated and marked her, I had to tell her what I was, that not just me, but everyone on the ranch were shifters. Audrey hadn't told her, that was for fucking sure.

Yeah, Marina had a mate, not just a man in her

life. Unfortunately, I couldn't just bite her and be done with it. She thought I was heading back to base, to pick up my weapon and head out on the next tour. I'd outright told her I was going back.

She was twenty-fucking-one years old. She had her whole life ahead of her. College. When I was her age, I'd already finished my first tour and seen shit I'd never forget. Hell, based on the way she'd responded, she'd barely fucked.

With my wolf hearing, I knew Rob was in his office. I went down the front stairs, took a right and went into the space that had belonged to my dad.

Rob looked up from his work at the big desk. "I'm surprised you're conscious."

I used to sit across from my dad while he worked —in the spot where Rob was now—listening to his conversations as I built Legos. I knew I wasn't ever going to be alpha, not with Rob being older, but I'd always liked to hear how my father dealt with issues and problems. I liked to think I used those skills when dealing with my soldiers under my command.

He smirked and sat back in his chair.

"She's mine," I snarled.

He held up his hands. "We figured that out, that's for damn sure. It's not me you have to win over."

"Boyd," I murmured, realizing I was in trouble

with him. I scratched the back of my neck, thinking of the bro code about dating sisters. Or fucking them.

I was so sated, my muscles so lax from having my balls drained, not once, but twice. I was at my most easygoing. If Boyd wanted to punch me in the face, now was the time to do it. Because I wasn't just fucking Marina into unconsciousness. Well, I was, but not just to empty my balls. She was my mate, and he was going to have to get used to the idea. Double time.

"You fucked his almost sister-in-law." Rob crossed his arms and leaned back in his chair. Clearly, we were thinking along the same lines.

"I fucked my mate, who just happens to be his almost sister-in-law," I clarified. "You'd have done the same."

He dipped his head once in agreement.

"I'll talk to him."

"No need. He's coming."

I heard his footsteps a split second after Rob.

Boyd came into the office, shutting the door behind him. Then he punched me in the gut. Twice. *Hard.*

I let him. I probably could've taken him, given

him a solid run. We were equally matched strength-wise, but I had ten years of training in hand-to-hand combat, and his best skill was staying on a crazy bull. Still, I figured I deserved it. My gut clenched in agony now, but shifters healed almost immediately, so a punch between brothers was easily taken.

"You know how old that girl is, Colton?" he asked on a snarl.

I coughed a little because he'd knocked the wind out of me. "Twenty-one."

"That's right." Boyd put his hands on his hips and nodded, his hat dipping in time with his head. "Twenty-one and still in fucking college. I don't know what the fuck you're thinking, but—"

"I'm thinking she's my mate," I countered. "No, not thinking. I *know* she's my mate."

He stared at me, wide eyed, then took off his hat and scratched his head. "Fuck." He spat the curse in a short, punctuated syllable as he swung around to face away from me and stare up at the ceiling. "Fate's a fucking whore, isn't she?"

"I don't know, you seem pretty fucking happy with the mate she sent you," I countered, finally able to stand upright again. I rubbed my stomach. "It wasn't all that long ago you found Audrey. You remember this feeling. Like a sucker punch to the gut."

Yeah, that had double meaning, and he glared at me. Then his face softened for a moment, as if just thinking about Audrey could change his entire mood. Shaking his head, he pointed a stern finger at me, like he was suddenly the oldest brother and not the sorry pest who ran around here sulking for years on end because he wasn't old enough to shift and run with us yet.

"She's not ready for you," he warned. "Jesus, you kill people for a living, and she's just a coed."

I ground my molars. I might actually have agreed with Boyd, but I sure as fuck didn't like anyone telling me to back off my own mate. "I know," I growled. "I told her as much. She's young. I'm a jaded military man. What makes you the fucking expert on my mate?" I shot back.

"I know she's still in college and practically a virgin. Or at least she was before you got a hold of her." Boyd's sourness stirred shame in my chest. "I had to drag Audrey from the house, so we didn't have to listen to you two."

Had I just corrupted an innocent? She definitely hadn't been a virgin last night. The way she'd acted, it was as if she'd let her inner wild girl out instead of being experienced. I'd guided her to come from a man's touch, and she'd let me. Hell, she submitted so fucking beautifully.

The vision of Marina tied up in my bed upstairs, her pink center weeping for my cock, her sweet lips begging me for release, rose up in my mind. My cock rose, too.

No, she'd wanted it. But that didn't mean she wanted me. As in for keeps.

Once a wolf mated, it was for life. There was no such thing as divorce. A female could leave her mate, but if he'd marked her, he'd never let her go. He'd be compelled to follow her to all ends of the Earth and watch over her. Ensure she was protected, provided for, and kept safe. He might be restrained enough to keep a distance, maybe even ignore it if she took another lover, but he'd never let go. It would be a biological impossibility.

"She's my *mate*," I growled through clenched teeth. Those three words should've been enough to convince any shifter male she belonged to me. Whether the timing sucked right now or not. "She was standing in the middle of a fucking storm watching the creek flood over the road. I thought she might do something stupid and cross."

"Instead she did you." Rob's lips twitched as he said it.

Boyd spun around and growled at him.

Grinning, I added, "I knew the second I breathed her in."

That's what sealed the deal. Boyd knew what it was like. I knew he did. He couldn't argue with his wolf, and neither could I.

I was past thirty. Already feeling the pull of moon madness coming on because I hadn't found and marked a female. It had been affecting my work for a while, which meant it affected my men. I was a liability to my team and one of the reasons I was on leave. I'd left to decide if I should even re-up because the last thing I wanted to do was get people killed by my negligence. I hadn't expected to find my mate though. Now, I had to decide what to do with Marina in mind. There was no decision. I wasn't going back. But she was.

"I'm running out of time." I looked at Rob, who knew what I meant. He was two years older than I was. He had to have been affected by moon madness. Hell, I'd be surprised if he wasn't already going half-feral.

Rob stood up from the desk and walked around,

folding his arms across his chest. "So, what's your plan, Colton?"

An anvil-like weight settled down on my chest. "Fuck if I know," I admitted.

Boyd opened his mouth, but Rob held up a hand, and he instantly fell silent at our alpha's command. "Let him talk it through, Boyd."

Him meant me. Well, fuck.

That meant Rob expected me to arrive at the right decision on my own. Marina was my mate, so he wouldn't be stupid enough to try to tell me anything. Even a directive from an alpha might not take with a male if it concerned his mate. Especially one with some moon madness in him.

Mark her, my wolf growled.

But Boyd and Rob were standing there as my judges and jury. Was it the right thing to do? Change the course of a young human's life before she'd even had a chance to figure out what she wanted for herself?

What about college? Her degree? Was I going to ask her to give that up for me, especially with only one year left? For what? To be a military wife on base? To be my little ranch wife here in Cooper Valley? Was either option fair to her?

Fuck.

It took all my effort, but I shoved my wolf's mounting agitation down. He wanted her claimed and made mine immediately. No, he'd wanted it done the night before.

I swallowed hard over the invisible band closing around my throat. "I have to wait." The words nearly made me sick to say. "Until she's done with school. Maybe re-up to keep me from going fucking nuts, although that'll be a fucking cluster. I'm struggling with the need to shift and run, and it's not going to ease up. It'll probably only get worse." I shrugged.

"You're saying not bite and claim her? That's insane. You'll rage through and kill the enemy single handedly," Rob commented drily.

"I could retire, stay here to run off the pressure while she finishes her last year," I added. I liked that idea a bit better. It was safer for everyone, except me. She'd probably come here to visit Audrey, who I imagined would soon be knocked up, if she wasn't already. Shit, that wouldn't make it any easier.

Rob nodded. "That sounds reasonable." He looked to Boyd, who also grudgingly nodded. "Maybe you should claim her now, though, to take the pressure off."

"No fucking way," Boyd snapped. "She's barely an adult! You can't saddle her with a lifetime commitment at her age. It's not fair. She doesn't even know what you are."

A growl filled the room. It took me a minute to realize it was coming from me. From my wolf. Both my brothers tensed, like I was about to go feral and attack them.

"What do you think?" Rob asked, eyeing me, keeping his voice neutral. I knew I was being handled by him, and it pissed me the fuck off, but it also worked. Him forcing me to make the right decision ensured I would do it. And would take away any pissing contest between me and the two of them.

That didn't mean the growling stopped. In fact, I went to speak and had to clear my throat to get words out.

"It's fucking impossible not to bite her. But I won't. I can't do it. Maybe when she gets closer to graduation. Next year."

Fuck, my wolf wanted to rip my throat out at what I was suggesting.

"Makes sense," Rob rumbled. "But completely unrealistic. There's no way you'll survive. Having her here, fucking her, then letting her go? Impossible."

"Yeah, there's no way." Fucking Boyd.

"It's not up to you," I snarled, suddenly ready for that fight.

Rob stepped between us. "He's just looking out for Audrey and what's important to her." He looked to me. "You have to let her go. Now. The full moon's tomorrow night. Taking her again is risky, at best."

The idea of not sinking into her soft body made me clench my fists. I hated what Rob was saying, but he was right. I was struggling now. What would I do tomorrow? I'd claim her and ruin everything. My wolf disagreed, thought it would make everything right.

"Fuck!" I shouted. I wanted Marina. I could scent her on me. Taste her. She was in my fucking bed right now. "I won't touch her. Fine. It was a fling. at least that's what she'll think. It's what she was looking for anyway."

The words tasted like poison in my mouth. I was lying to myself, and I'd have to lie to her.

"Jesus, brother. You might save lives in the army, but this? You're a fucking martyr," Rob said, shaking his head.

I rubbed a hand over the back of my neck. Paced. "I'm doing it for my *mate*."

Boyd looked to Rob and laughed. "Fifty bucks says he makes it a day."

Rob nodded.

They were taking bets I wouldn't be able to hold

out. The fuckers. I had to hold off. Biting her now wasn't an option. College. Life. It had to happen for her. I could hold off.

I could.

I would.

9

Marina

I woke up to the scent of meat on a grill.

Looking at the bedside clock, I saw I'd slept until dinnertime. Between the sex and the talking, I hadn't slept much the night before. And then this afternoon... wow. I guessed that was what a good orgasm would do to you. My body was purring, still languid, warm and satisfied. And yes, a bit sore in some places, but I didn't mind a bit.

Thank you, Colton.

I slid out of his bed and pulled on my clothes to find a shower. I was sure I looked like a holy mess—

and well fucked—since Colton met me. Last night, a drowned rat. Today, a flour covered baker. It was silly, but I wanted to put a little effort into my appearance for him. He'd seen more of me naked than dressed. I giggled.

I made it quick, though, since I heard the clamor of voices in the kitchen downstairs. I didn't want to miss dinner entirely. I ducked into the bathroom down the hall, showered, then slipped on a short, strappy sundress that showed off my legs and shoulders. There was no time to blow dry my hair, but I rubbed some lip gloss between my lips and put on some sparkly sandals before I ran down the back stairs.

I'd been right, a whole crew of people had gathered in the giant kitchen, and most of them turned when I came down. I swore a few of the men lifted their noses in the air and sniffed, but that wouldn't make sense. Colton had done that the night before, but I mentally shrugged it off as crazy.

"Hey everyone." I threw my arms wide as a greeting. "I'm Marina, Audrey's little sister."

"Yes, you are," Colton rumbled. I hadn't seen him because he'd been standing in the corner, but he immediately moved forward to flank me. He started to reach one hand toward my lower back but then retracted it, as if he didn't want to touch me.

After what we just did, I wouldn't think it would be a problem. Maybe he was against PDA or something.

His large body blocked everyone else out. He whispered, "Do you ever wear a bra?" I don't know why he sounded grumpy about it.

His gaze dipped to my chest, and I shook my head.

"You're wearing panties under that little dress, right?"

I pulled my lips to the side and shrugged my shoulders, playing coy.

He growled.

God, it felt good to know I affected him.

I'd fallen asleep on him, too worn out from his dominance and skill to remain conscious. He should feel proud of himself because even hours later, I felt well fucked. Still, my doubts flared. This was a fling. I had to remember that. Getting too hungry for this man's attention was a bad idea. The last guy I'd been with had done a number on me, fucked me and moved on. Then there was dear old Dad, never showing any interest at all. Ugh, I had issues. And yet, Colton seemed like he wanted to offer... more. Did he? I couldn't read him.

Audrey was at the other end of the kitchen, nestled against her fiancé. She smiled broadly and waved at me. A stab of guilt went through me, remembering how I'd pretty much abandoned her and the unfinished wedding cake. She must have cleaned up while Colton and I had been... busy.

"I'm sorry about abandoning the cake," I said to her.

She waved her hand through the air. "I put it all away for later. No worries."

I was here for her, not to spend all my time in bed with a hot military man. He'd changed out of his cargo pants and t-shirt for jeans and a plaid, cotton snap shirt. He wasn't just a military man but a cowboy, too.

I looked Audrey's way once again, realizing I was again distracted by virile manliness. Ugh.

I'd make it up to her tonight for the surprise bachelorette party. Becky, one of Audrey's friends from the hospital, had contacted me about planning Audrey's last hurrah as a single woman. I told her by email Audrey wouldn't want anything fancy, so we were just going with a night at Cody's, the local—and as I understood—*only* watering hole in Cooper

Valley. The surprise part was a limo Becky managed to rent that would be picking us up in a couple hours.

I had told Audrey I wanted some sister-time with her tonight, so she shouldn't have anything scheduled. Well, at least I was rested up for the fun.

"Sleep well?" Colton asked. He still sounded grouchy. Still wasn't touching me.

"So well." I rotated to face him, tipped my chin up and grinned. "I guess I have you to thank for that."

Something flickered in his expression, but I couldn't decipher it. His brown eyes almost glowed gold the way the light from the windows hit them. He took one of those strange deep breaths. "You washed off my scent."

"What?" I wrinkled my nose, not quite understanding. Was that a thing? Guys don't want you to shower after sex? I'd have to ask Audrey about it at the bachelorette party.

"Nothing. Nevermind."

Damn. Somebody didn't get a nap. You'd think he'd be chipper after screwing me six ways until Sunday.

Just then Rob carried a giant—and it was *giant*—platter of steaks in from the back deck, and the focus shifted to food. On the table, there was a big casserole dish heaped with baked potatoes wrapped in foil and a plate piled with chopped celery and carrots.

Colton hung by my side, not touching me, but staying close. He directed me over to the table, giving me all the ranch hands' names as we passed them. Johnny, Levi, Clint.

"So nice to meet you," I kept saying, but he didn't give me a chance to stop and shake hands. "We need name tags." I laughed as he pulled out a chair for me, then settled next to me. "I'm afraid I won't remember everyone."

"Only one name you need to remember, little girl." Colton leaned into me as he forked a steak from the platter and put it on my plate.

"Oh yeah?" I murmured in a voice I hoped was only loud enough for him to hear. "Is it the one I was screaming all afternoon?"

"Christ, Marina." He stared down at me with bald hunger. "How the fuck am I gonna keep my hands off you?"

I frowned at him, and my heart gave a little lurch. "Why... why do you have to?"

The screen door slapped and broke our connection as some of the ranch hands took their piled high plates and headed outside to eat, leaving the three brothers, Audrey and me sitting around the large table. Two of the ranch hands, Levi and—dammit, I'd already forgotten the other one's name joined us.

"Colton, I was certainly not expecting you to steal my sister away from me this week," Audrey said, her voice slightly scolding, but the smile on her face softened it.

I clapped a hand over my mouth. "I'm so sorry! Of course, I've come here for you."

"It sounded like you came for Colton," Rob murmured. Levi laughed, but covered it with his napkin.

Colton shot them both death glares, even though he'd been perfectly plain about what we'd done when he arrived.

Audrey gasped and threw a roll at her future brother-in-law. Rob easily caught it and took a bite, smirking.

I wanted the floor to open up.

"I'm here for you," I clarified, saying the words slowly and eyeing Rob even though they were meant for Audrey. *Except for when I was tied to Colton's bed.* Shit. "I promise I'll be more present the rest of the week."

"Yeah, you're here for Audrey," Colton added.

I looked at Audrey although I was confused by him. So... it was sex and punishment for leaving and now... over? I shook that away. "We're having sister time, tonight, remember?" My words rushed out in one breath. "In the morning, I'll finish the cake. I promise."

The layers were all baked, but I hadn't gotten to the frosting. I could finish that and the flower decorations in the morning.

Audrey waved her hand. "I'm just teasing. Rob, obviously, too. I'm thrilled you and Colton hit it off. You both deserve your fun. What's the plan for tonight, anyway?"

I smiled broadly and waggled my brows as I cut a piece of meat. "You'll find out soon enough!"

"Uh oh," Audrey said, her eyes narrowed behind her glasses. "What am I missing? Why do you look so excited? Oh God, please tell me you didn't arrange for a stripper-gram."

"Maybe I did," I tucked a bite of steak in my mouth and then moaned because it was the juiciest thing I've ever tasted. "This is so good."

Beside me, Colton shifted in his chair and gave a low, animalistic growl.

I had no idea what could've gotten into him since this afternoon.

"Yeah, Rob's great on the grill," Boyd said to me, then looked pointedly at Audrey. "Let me tell you something, though, darlin'. There will be nobody stripping for my bride but me."

"No strippers," Colton agreed, his voice a deep velvet right by my ear. He set a baked potato on my plate as he did so. For someone who seemed disgruntled, he was also being very attentive.

I didn't get it.

"Relax, boys." I held up my hand. "I did not hire a stripper to come out to the ranch."

"Tell me you didn't hire one, period," Colton warned.

"I didn't hire one, period." I rolled my eyes. "Now, stop. I'm terrible at keeping secrets when I get excited, and I don't want to give it away."

"Hmm," Audrey said, but she was sweet enough to let it drop. She'd probably already figured it out. She was a smart woman, my sister.

10

Colton

I FUCKING HATED SURPRISES. I knew it made me a control freak, but in my line of work, surprises meant someone could get killed. We drilled and drilled, so we never had surprises.

Over ten years in the military, and one pint-sized woman ruined it all. At least it wasn't life or death, unless some guy looked overlong at my mate in that sundress. Still, watching Marina bubble with excitement over her plans for the evening made it impossible for me to complain. She was so fucking adorable. Her happiness would be contagious if I wasn't so sick with need for her and trying to keep my hands off her.

And the ranch hands away. Johnny was close to her age and would be on her like bees to a flower. I knew I was being insane, but I didn't want any of the guys to think they had a chance, and that had meant sticking close to her through dinner. There was no doubt they could scent me on her, but I hadn't marked her. She was still fair game, if they fucking dared.

The hottest female on the planet had just been in my bed. I should have zero complaints. But I'd just resolved not to touch her for a fucking year. I'd made it two hours. I wasn't sure if I could make it. Then I thought of Boyd's bet. The fucker.

I might not be able to touch her, but letting her go out on the town without my protection was an impossibility. That was never going to fucking happen.

When we heard the crunch of gravel out on the drive, and Johnny appeared in the kitchen saying there was a limo out front, the first words out of my mouth were, "Oh, hell no."

"Excuse me?" Marina demanded, putting her hands on her hips and lifting a defiant face up to mine. It made me want to fold her over the table, pull up that short dress spank her until she squealed. And she'd like it, too. Of course, in that fantasy of mine, we'd be alone in the kitchen, and it would end with me pleasuring her in every possible way with her sprawled out on the center island.

Fuck—I had to stop thinking with my dick!

"A limo?" Audrey popped out of her chair and ran for the front door. Marina followed.

I cleared my throat, looking to Boyd for help. I knew he couldn't possibly want that giant black stretch limo taking his female away from him for the night, especially when they were getting married tomorrow.

Boyd and I had a brief and silent conversation across the table. It may have been a while since I'd seen him, but we had clearly melded minds because he stood up and strode down the hall to the front door announcing, "Only way you two ladies get in that limo is if we come, too."

I followed.

Marina turned to face me on the porch and rolled her eyes. "You can't. It's a bachelorette party! For *women*. No strippers. Just fun. Come on, we have to take the bride out on the town. It's tradition."

It was a pretty summer night, the weather calm in comparison to the night before. At least I didn't have to worry about that, although storms blew in on summer evenings often enough. It wasn't just last night that was a stark reminder of that, but my parents had been killed in the canyon during a storm. Boyd had barely made it out.

Fuck, I was losing my shit. Since when did I worry about the *weather?*

A couple other ladies had climbed out of the limo, made those high-pitched squeals of feminine happiness and had hustled Audrey inside to put a rhinestone-bedazzled "Bride" tee and a tiara on her. Boyd and I stared from the front porch.

Fucking ridiculous, this human tradition. And we'd just said we were going with them. Yeah, I was officially insane.

"I'm so winning that fifty bucks," Boyd murmured, then slapped me on the back before hopping in the back of the limo.

The women were inside laughing and prepping except for Marina. It seemed she was letting Audrey have fun with her girlfriends. She stuck her head in the open door. "Seriously? The kitchen table's still covered with food. You're just going to leave it all?"

Boyd shrugged. "Rob's not coming. He'll take care of it."

She didn't look too happy to have that issue—

excuse—resolved. "You guys." She glanced around the dim interior. "There won't be room for all of us with you in here."

"Audrey can ride on Boyd's lap," I said stubbornly, trying to erase the image of her grinding over *my* lap the entire ride, that short dress riding up to show more thigh.

I shook my head again. Fuck. The full moon was approaching, and it had me all-consumed with her. It had never been like this although I'd never had my mate during one before. I was fucking doomed.

"Guys, really. This is a women-only event."

"Sorry, darlin'. I'm afraid this is a non-negotiable. Colton and I can't let you ladies go out unescorted. We'd go nuts back here imagining all the low-lifes who would get to see you while we couldn't. You wouldn't want us to suffer like that."

I was grateful to Boyd for arguing the case because I was incapable of saying anything coherent at the moment. Not when her vanilla and cinnamon scent filled the limo, making my senses go haywire.

"Fine, you can come," she relented, as if she had any choice. "We're not doing anything crazy, just going to a bar called Cody's," she explained to Boyd, as if that might make us change our minds about accompanying them. "The limo's so we can stay safe."

Boyd winked at her. "Darlin', I know you love her, too, but nobody takes my wife out without me around to protect her."

"She'll hardly be in any danger," Marina protested.

"She gets tired easily these days and—" Boyd snapped his mouth shut.

"*Why* does she get tired easily these days?" Marina demanded, one pale brow arched.

It took me a moment longer to read into Boyd's words. But when he quickly shook his head and said, "Nevermind," I understood.

Boyd and Audrey had been keeping news from us. She was having a pup. It didn't surprise me in the least. They were already mated. They'd been together about two months now, and he'd claimed her, bitten her and all, about a week in. If they fucked at a pace anything like what I wanted to do with Marina, then it was practically impossible for Audrey not to be pregnant.

"Oh my God!" Marina squealed, climbing in the limo and flashing those bare thighs as she did. Which only wanted me to flip up that cute dress and get a baby in her, right fucking now. "I'm so excited to be an auntie!"

"What's this about becoming an auntie?" one of the other women demanded as she climbed in the limo. Two other ladies followed, all three introducing themselves. Becky, Anna and Leigh. They worked at the hospital with Audrey. I guessed them to be Audrey's age or thereabouts. They were attractive in their western wear, yet my wolf could care less. I couldn't, either, not with a sweet thing like Marina as comparison.

Marina had been right. There wasn't room for us in the limo. As the women scooted and squeezed, it became apparent we weren't all going to fit.

"Um, either you need to leave, or I'm sitting on your lap," Marina informed me.

My dick got hard again. It was turning into a permanent state around her, which wasn't helping my situation. "I'm not leaving."

"Your choice," she sang out, obviously not disappointed in the least to drop her perfect ass in my lap.

It was all I could do not to stroke everywhere—up and down her bare thighs, under that short dress, between her little tits. Somehow, I managed to only wrap an arm around her waist and pull her soft buttocks over my rigid cock.

Blue balls.

I was going to be in a permanent state of blue balls this week.

How in the fuck could I avoid this little human when my brain had permanently traveled south to reside in my dick?

Audrey climbed in last, the sparkly tiara holding her long hair back from her face. She looked happy —as usual with Boyd—but excited, too. This was a special time for her, and I was glad she had her friends with her to celebrate. But I wasn't letting any of these ladies go to Cody's without a chaperone. They were all too pretty, too sweet, to not be hounded by dicks with... dicks. That place was a meat market, guys on the prowl for fresh meat. Audrey had an obvious "Taken" sign on her with the tiara and t-shirt, but Marina... they'd be ready to gobble her up.

"I'm sorry, darlin'. I didn't tell her, she guessed." Boyd reached for his bride and settled her on his lap before the limo glided into motion. He nuzzled a kiss at her neck and the arm wrapped around her settled low on her flat belly.

Audrey's other friends let out a chorus of squeals and congratulations, which Audrey tried to quell. "Don't tell anyone at the hospital," she warned. "It's early days. I don't want to make it public until the second trimester." She was an Ob/Gyn and knew what she was talking about.

She looked up at Boyd. "I won't be riding the bull tonight."

He nipped at the spot where he'd claimed her. "The mechanical bull? Hell, no. You'll ride me instead, and I promise you'll have just as much fun."

Audrey giggled, and the other ladies fanned themselves.

"We can have this limo just take us up to our cabin, and you can have your bull now."

Audrey tried to work herself off her mate's lap. "Oh no. I might not be able to drink, but I can still have some fun."

"I'm so happy, Audrey." Marina laid her hand on her sister's arm. This time her voice was choked with tears.

I squeezed her. I couldn't help it. She was such an exuberant thing. So full of laughter, life, and emotion. I hadn't realized how one-dimensional and boring I'd become in the military. Next to her, I was like a stone man. She was colorful light.

"I hope I'm not ruining the party. No mechanical bulls, no drinks," Audrey promised with a smile.

"I'll drink for you," Becky offered, the other ladies nodding in agreement, laughing.

"We have more to celebrate now," Marina declared. "Just because you're pregnant, doesn't mean you can't dance."

"Mmm, Cody's isn't much of a dance place," Leigh said. "But we'll figure something out."

The idea of Marina dancing in that flirty little dress made me groan.

I seriously wasn't going to make it through the night.

An hour later, I was nearing death. Somehow, Bossy Becky, as I now thought of her, had cleared a section of the bar, and the ladies, along with some other fun-loving patrons, were line dancing. I didn't give a shit about any of them, but I did about Marina and the way her dress swirled with every turn. I saw higher and higher on her pale thighs, and that meant every other fucker in the bar saw too.

Our convo from earlier about whether she was wearing panties made me want to rip out every man's eyeballs. If I was wondering, then they sure as fuck were too.

"I'm impressed," Boyd said, standing beside me. We were leaning against the wall between the pool tables and the bathrooms with a clear view of the ladies. The country music pulsed through the hidden speakers in tempo with the throbbing in my temples.

He took a pull from his beer bottle. I held mine but hadn't touched more than a few sips.

"With what?" I asked, my eyes on my mate.

"That you haven't dragged her out of there."

Two women walked past toward the ladies' room, and I lost sight of Marina. I wanted to shove the women along... which meant I was losing my shit.

When I saw her again, all of two seconds later, she moved two steps to the right, in sync with the others, then did a spin, her skirt flaring up.

"Fuck," I said to myself. Boyd laughed. "Your woman's out there, too."

"Yeah, but mine's wearing jeans and not showing off all of her—"

I turned to him. "Don't fucking say it."

He held up his hands in front of him, beer held in one. "Mine's got my mark on her neck and my baby in her belly. You're keeping your hands off."

I growled, pissed. Yeah, Boyd was the messenger, but still. I had *nothing* to tie Marina to me other than my wolf saying she belonged to me. She belonged out there, having fun, having guys ogle her fucking gorgeous legs. That was what twenty-one year olds did. The smile on her face and the flush to her cheeks showed how much fun she was having. Audrey was next to her, and they were laughing.

There was nothing inappropriate about their fun. The sundress covered more of Marina than some of the outfits other women were wearing. She wasn't even looking at other guys.

Yet I wanted to toss her over my shoulder and carry her out of there. If I did, everyone in the bar would get a show of that taut ass that belonged to me.

I ran a hand over my face, and Boyd slapped me on the shoulder. "Welcome to the club, brother. I'm going to enjoy spending that fifty bucks."

Fuck. *Fuck.*

I couldn't have her, and I couldn't leave her alone.

When a guy, more her age than mine, joined her and started dancing along beside her, I saw red. My wolf wanted to rip the fucker's head off.

I took a step forward, but Boyd's hand on my arm stopped me. "Easy."

Looking his way, I practically snarled at him. "Easy for you to say. Your woman's wearing fucking jeans."

With that, I was off. Marina might not be mine, but she definitely wasn't for that pansy ass in the Wranglers. If she wanted to get it on with a guy, it was going to be me. Except I couldn't do a fucking thing about it.

Fuck.

11

Marina

I HAD no idea line dancing could be so much fun. Becky and the other ladies from the hospital were hilarious and could cut a rug as if they were in a country dance competition. And they were super cute in their jeans and cowgirl boots. Leigh was even worse with a fun cowboy hat with braids. Audrey wasn't much better than me, but she was having the best time, too, even decked out in the silly t-shirt and tiara.

This was why I'd come to Montana. To hang with my sister, to cut loose. Well, I'd cut loose all right, but with Colton, which was a whole lot of fun in a completely different way. As I spun with the others, I caught a glimpse of Colton and Boyd. They were watching us. Of course, they were.

I should have been upset they felt we needed keepers, but I had to admit, the way they were looking from their spot against the wall was more like two possessive men than babysitters. They gave us room, but it was obvious they were there with us. They blended in with the crowd at Cody's. Both of them screamed cowboy. Boyd, with the cowboy hat I wondered if he even wore to bed and that huge rodeo championship belt buckle. Colton wasn't wearing a hat, and his well- worn jeans and snug shirt were just like everyone else's. It was the way he carried himself, the way his gaze roved over the space as if keeping watch for any kinds of dangers, that set him apart.

There were cute guys everywhere. I might have been young, but I wasn't stupid. I knew who flirted with me. But none of them were Colton. Sure, some guys were closer to my age than him, but they just seemed like boys. Just like the guys back at college. I wondered if they would spank me or tie me up. I wondered if they'd make me call them *sir* when naked. I didn't think so. I didn't think I'd get wet for them either. None of them would compare to Colton. None of them *did*.

That was why, when the song was over, it was Colton my nipples got hard for as he cut through the crowd to get to me. Ever since I woke up from my nap, I'd gotten mixed signals from him. He'd barely touched me, but he couldn't stop looking at me. He'd been watching me like a hawk since we got to the bar, and now he was heading my way. I licked my lips, wishing he'd carry me off like he had earlier in his kitchen.

But this was Audrey's bachelorette party. No matter how many orgasms I craved, they'd have to wait.

"Hey," I said. He stood so close our bodies almost touched, his hot from... from him being *hot*. His gaze was almost penetrating, reminding me of when he'd lifted me down from the sign by the swollen creek. As if I was the only person in the world. He sniffed, then growled. Or I thought it was a growl over the music.

"Let's get a drink."

I nodded. He reached for my elbow, but like earlier, seemed to rethink it and just held out an ushering hand to indicate the path to the end of the bar. I looked back, and Audrey and Boyd were right behind us. Boyd talked a guy off a stool and set it before Audrey, so she could sit. I hadn't gotten used to the idea that Audrey was pregnant.

The kind of family I'd always wanted—two people who loved each other obsessively having a baby that would be the center of their world—was right in front of me. Growing. I was crazily jealous of what she had, but she deserved it. After my dad being a dick and ditching her mom and Audrey having to pretty much raise herself *and* take care of her depressed mom... Yeah, the tiara she wore should have been made of diamonds.

I leaned my side against the bar, and Colton loomed beside me, his foot resting on the brass rail as he flagged down the bartender.

"Where are the others?" I asked.

Audrey tilted her head, the tiara teetering a bit as she did so, and looked around. Raising her arm, she pointed toward the back. I had no idea how I missed Becky on top of the mechanical bull. It was whipping her back and forth, but she was holding on, her free hand swinging over her head. I couldn't see Leigh or Anna in the crowd, but I assumed they were with her.

"She's a riot," I told Audrey.

She nodded, pushing her glasses up. "Amazing

nurse, too. She's much better at riding that bull than I am."

"You rode it?" I asked, staring at my staid sister and back at Becky who was whooping it up. "Why have I never heard about this?"

"She was pretty good, too," Boyd said, kissing Audrey's temple.

Audrey grinned but rolled her eyes. "One time," she clarified. "Well, my days of bull riding are like Boyd's. Over."

The bartender came by with bottles of water and set them before us. Colton screwed off a cap and handed one to me. I frowned at it. "I wanted another lemon drop," I said. I wasn't planning on getting drunk, but it wasn't a bachelorette party without a little alcohol. "I'm drinking for Audrey."

Just then, the waiter came back with my preferred drink—which showed Colton had been watching me closely—and a Shirley Temple, which Audrey grabbed right up and pulled a cherry from the glass and popped it in her mouth.

"You'll have your drink, but the water, too."

Well. I guess he did have a Daddy streak in him. Bossy, but sweet.

I took my drink and looked up at him through

my lashes. I had no idea how to respond to that other than, *okay* or *yes, please,* so I stayed quiet.

"So, Colton, when do you have to be back to base?" Audrey asked.

I stilled, and I felt oddly deflated. I hadn't forgotten this was temporarily, but I wanted to. He was going back to North Carolina. I only had a few weeks until fall semester started... in a different time zone. On the opposite side of the country from him. In no fantasy world could I imagine that what we started this week could become anything. At least not right now.

"Next week," he replied.

"Boyd told me you might not re-enlist." She swirled her drink around with her straw.

Colton glanced at his brother. "Did he?"

"Are you?" I asked, curious. We may have done things a little backward, having sex first and the whole getting-to-know-you thing second. It was probably a good idea to see where he stood on the priority of his career. I assumed, like most people, it was pretty high. "Leaving the military?"

He gave a negligent shrug, as if it wasn't a huge decision. "There might be another tour in me."

"To Afghanistan?" My mouth was suddenly dry. From our little middle of the night chat at the motel,

I knew he'd been deployed before. Multiple times. The basis for that nightmare. Why would he want to go back if he had a chance to retire? He wasn't old, but still...

"Wherever they send us. What about you? You've got one year left of school."

It was my turn to shrug. "Yeah, but there's no threat of the enemy or IED in the engineering department."

"Coming to Montana's a vacation for both of you," Audrey replied. "I'm just glad you could be here." She leaned toward me. "Maybe we'll do some line dancing tomorrow night at the reception."

"Hell, no. We agreed to the wedding," Boyd said, picking up Audrey's left hand and kissing the engagement ring. "And one hour at the reception. Then I get you all to myself."

"We agreed on two hours," she countered. "Besides, we've already made the baby you said you were going to put in me... tomorrow night."

"I can't help it if I'm so potent."

"It's that Wolf blood," I said.

Audrey's and Boyd's heads whipped my way so fast I thought they'd get whiplash. Colton's body tensed against mine. What had I said wrong? Glancing up at Colton, I asked, "What?"

"What do you mean, *wolf?*" he asked, his voice slow.

I frowned. "That's your last name, isn't it?"

The corner of his mouth tipped up, and he exhaled. "Sure is."

Boyd laughed and took a swig of his beer. Audrey brought her drink to her lips and sucked on the straw. I looked between them, wondered what was up.

Becky, Leigh and Anna invaded then. Boyd and Colton stepped back for us to make a small circle around Audrey.

"I am so excited for their baby," I said to Colton.

He inched back from me when I moved closer. He kept sniffing me. Did I smell bad?

Ouch. Was he no longer interested?

No, that was impossible. I'd felt how hard he was for me riding on his lap over here. He *stared.*

It must be the PDA thing. Right?

"You want babies?" Colton asked, his eyes dark.

"I'm excited for *their* baby. I'm not interested in my own baby right now… or anytime soon."

Colton made even more space between us. "Right. You're young. You've got your whole life ahead of you. Life in the big city, a job at an engineering firm."

All of a sudden, and perhaps because it was Colton who said it aloud, it sounded awful. I'd finish my degree, definitely, but the thought of living in LA, perpetually stuck in traffic to get to a dry job inspecting bridges or construction plans... gah.

I wanted what Audrey had. A man to look at me like Boyd did Audrey. How he treated her like something precious, yet I knew their love life was anything but tame. Tame and wild, that was Audrey.

I felt like I had that, at least the start of it... the framework of it, with Colton. The connection was undeniable. The heat. Maybe it was the way the Wolf brothers were raised, but I liked it when Colton took charge. In bed and out. I liked that he felt the need to watch over me even at the bar. Even when he acted grumpy about it. As if he didn't dare let me out of his sight.

I wanted everything with him, but it wasn't even an option. He had made it clear he was a military man. Stationed across the country, he was devoted to his men, being a leader. Taking their training, their lives seriously. Going to *war*. Why would he give that up for me?

He wouldn't. I'd made it clear it was just a fling when I'd seduced him in the motel room. He'd agreed and seemed to be Mr. Hands Off now. End of story. I'd gotten exactly what I wanted. And that felt pretty crappy.

"Come on!" Becky cried, and tugged Audrey off her stool so fast, she practically tossed her drink at Boyd.

"Let's go, Marina," Anna said, her shoulders shifting with the beat of the music. "Ooh, I love this song. Time to dance some more. It's time for *The Git Up* dance. You'll pick it up quickly."

I set my drink on the bar and tagged along behind the others, giving one last glance at Colton before the crowd blocked him from view.

It was better this way. I was here for Audrey, and this was our night. Colton and I were here for the wedding, but that was all. Sure, he'd tied me down and fucked me hard only a few hours earlier, but I couldn't miss the *hands off* vibe now.

Oh my God. That was it. The sex earlier had been punishment. He'd even said as much. He'd spanked me and tortured me with edging for what felt like hours. He was getting back at me for what had happened in the motel room.

I'd seduced him, and he'd punished me for it. Sure, I'd loved the punishment, but it made sense. That was it with him. Payback had been a bitch. And incredible.

I'd felt it before. The end. Knew when it was over. I took a deep breath, pasted a smile on my face. This was Audrey's night. I couldn't be upset with something that had barely started.

I'd never get what Audrey and Boyd had. Not here. Not now. Not with Colton. I should thank him for showing me what I wanted from a guy in the sack. What I needed and craved and aim for that. I needed to focus on what was going to last, and that was my relationship with my sister, so I got in line beside them, ready to dance away Audrey's last night of being single. Go a little wild.

12

Colton

Once again, sleep had been impossible.

Knowing I couldn't possibly lay beside her without trying to mark her, I'd dropped her off at her guest bedroom last night with a kiss on the forehead when the limo had dropped us off.

I'd seen the hurt in her expression, then understanding. She knew I was rejecting her. She wasn't an idiot.

There was nothing to be done for it. I couldn't very well tell her I was dying to sink my teeth in her flesh.

That wouldn't go over well. Instead, she thought I was through with her.

Far fucking from it. Maybe once I'd mated her, I'd be able to rest. Fates, I hoped so. Until then... I was going to be stuck in fucking purgatory.

I guessed this was what moon madness was all about. The wolf in you started going fucking nuts because he hadn't claimed his mate. It felt worse than usual now, not only because it was a full moon in less than twelve hours but because she was under the same roof. Just down the fucking hall. Fuck, I could hear her tossing and turning.

Watching her at Cody's had been torture. Men had zeroed in on her, and I couldn't blame them. I'd wanted to rip their heads off, but Marina was a vision. Sassy, fun, lighthearted. She might be small, but she lit up a fucking room or an entire bar. And she hadn't been the one wearing the God-awful t-shirt and tiara.

Fuck, I ached. Needed. I would've thought finding her would make him calm down, but it was getting worse.

Hour by hour. Minute by minute. How was I going to handle this through the full moon much less for another school year?

All I could think about was fucking the lights out

of her and then sinking my teeth into that sweet flesh of hers at the nape of her neck. Having her come while I made her mine, filled her with my seed, marked her inside and out.

How had Boyd done it without endangering Audrey? He'd obviously been successful. But that was one of the reasons mating a human was forbidden. We didn't hurt women. Period. But when it came to this, there was no way around it. That was why Boyd was the only shifter I knew who had mated a human. It came from the old days, before modern medicine, when any kind of flesh wound might mean infection and death. That wasn't even considering the possibility of hitting a major artery and killing her right away. Humans were also off-limits due to the increased possibility of birthing a defective shifter—a pup who couldn't shift.

There was a time when I would've considered that the worst possible outcome. But here I was, dying to mate a human and put my pups in her belly. And if the halflings couldn't shift?

Well, that would be all right. As long as they were healthy and happy, I wouldn't give a shit. That meant I'd have Marina at my side where she belonged. Not across the fucking hall.

I wondered if Boyd felt the same about that halfling he was growing. I imagined he did.

Giving up on sleeping, I'd gone for a crack of dawn run—in human form—because we only let our wolves out up on the mountain. I'd pushed through ten miles and still felt like my head was going to pop off with the pent-up energy.

Heading upstairs to shower, I heard the alarm on Marina's cell chime through her closed bedroom door. That was followed by a groan.

She had to frost the cake and get it finished. That had been the excuse I used for not taking her to my room and fucking her raw again the night before. I'd seen it in her eyes. She hadn't believed me.

Yeah, I wouldn't have believed me either, especially when my dick had been a thick, unmistakable outline in my jeans.

I couldn't have sex with her again. No. NO! I needed to act normal, as if we'd had some fun, and now it was over. Talk. *Do* stuff. Clothed. It was the only way to make it through the full moon tonight without biting her and ruining her life.

I froze at the top of the stairs when I heard her coming out of her room. She wore a tank top—no bra—and a pair of red jean shorts that made me desperate to do all manner of dirty things to that ass of hers.

Don't look anywhere but her eyes.

"Good morning."

"Hi." She looked surprised to see me. Slightly flustered.

"You going down to the kitchen?"

"Um, yeah. I need to finish up the cake."

"Right. I'll help." What? What the fuck was I talking about? I knew jack shit about cakes.

"You will? Have you frosted a cake before?"

"Never," I admitted. "But I'm a quick learner. Or I can entertain you while you frost."

I could think of many ways to entertain her *with* frosting. All over her naked body.

Fuck. I groaned, and her eyes widened.

"Okay, Sergeant," she said.

"Sergeant Major," I corrected, watching her nipples go hard.

What did it? My rank? Or the bossy way I said it?

Either way, my mate had a thing for being dominated, which boded well for our future sex life... *after she graduated,* but at the moment made it hard for me to function.

I'd already jacked off twice last night, and this

morning before my run to let off some steam, but I was still hard for her. My new permanent state.

"I'm going to grab a quick shower, and then I'll join you."

She nodded and cut past me. I took a Navy shower, in and out in two minutes, and I was dressed and in the kitchen within five. Total.

There, I poured us both a cup of coffee from the full pot Rob must've made before he went out to do chores. "How about I make you breakfast?"

Providing. That was something a wolf mate knew how to do. It should resonate for a human, too. Right?

Her dimpled smile confirmed my instinct. "I'd love that." She moved with efficiency, pulling out a mixing bowl, butter and powdered sugar.

"What do you like?" I asked. "Pancakes? Eggs?"

"Whatever you're having," she said as she glanced at me over her shoulder.

"You're an easy one, huh?" I wanted to kiss the place where her neck met her collarbone. I wanted to get those red shorts off her hot little body.

No. *Breakfast.* Fuck!

"Give me a hint. What would make you moan in pleasure?"

Christ! Why are these things coming out of my mouth?

She had things to do. I needed to keep my hands off her and support her goals. In this case, I had to let her finish the cake.

"Pancakes, I guess. Or toast."

"Pancakes, it is." I was relieved to have direction. I was compiling my mental list: things that made Marina happy.

I rooted through my brother's refrigerator and pantry for ingredients. There was a huge bag of blueberries in the freezer as if a bear shifter had been to visit, so I pulled that out, too. "You like blueberries in your pancakes?" I asked, shutting the door behind me.

"Yum. Yes."

I wasn't sure how she made the simplest of words sound so damn sultry.

I whipped up a bowl of pancake batter—me standing on one side of the huge island and her on the other—and put a package of bacon in a pan because my wolf needed meat with every meal. While I worked, Marina flitted around the kitchen like a goddamn butterfly. So colorful and bright. She was efficient in her movements, pulling out the cake layers from the fridge, the metal spatula things. Based on the size of the cake plate, the final product wasn't going to be huge, but it would feed the twenty or so guests easily.

"I get that the...um, fling's over. No worries from me."

My wolf howled at me to say something, to tell her differently. But I couldn't. I froze and stared.

She looked away. My lack of reply was just as telling as if I'd said the words aloud.

"I'm cool. Just, um... tell me more about you, Colton Wolf," she declared, right before she stuck a finger of icing in her mouth.

My vision sharpened, telling me my eye color had probably changed. I blinked and looked away. My cock had punched out harder against my zipper. Fuck. I didn't know if it was hearing my name on her lips or seeing those very same lips close around her finger and wishing it was my cock that did it. Probably both.

I was close to losing control right here in the kitchen. Ripping her clothes off and claiming her in the roughest possible manner. Showing her the fling would never end. Showing her it wasn't a goddamn fling. But what could I say?

I'm a shifter, and I want to bite your neck and claim you so you can never leave me. Oh yeah, forget about college or any kind of dreams you may have had for yourself.

I cleared my throat. "What do you want to know?"

She washed her hands in the sink. "Everything."

My heart never lurched. I swear to fuck, my heart had never lurched in my life, not even in combat or when my parents had died. I was a wolf and a Green Beret. I didn't show nerves. But hearing that my little human wanted to know more about me seemed like a sign.

She was looking to fall in love. If she only wanted my dick, she'd have taken off that shirt and smeared frosting on her nipples and asked me to lick it off.

That was a fucking amazing albeit dangerous idea, but back to the point, her wanting love, I was well in the game here. Warmth seeped into my chest. Maybe we could... date. Shit. How did a guy do that?

"What's your favorite food?" she asked.

"Steak," I answered without thinking. "I'm a carnivore all the way. I grew up on a Montana ranch."

She'd set out the layers of cake, then placed rectangular sheets of paper on the cake plate, then set one of the tiers on top. Grabbing the spatula, she began to frost the first one. "Chocolate or vanilla?"

"Vanilla."

"Salty or sweet?"

"Hmm. Normally, I'd say salty, but you might change me on that."

She laughed, her eyes focused on the task. I flipped the bacon. "Why?"

"Because right now, I'm dying to try your cake. Or your frosting. Or, hell, anything you bake."

"Oh yeah?" she purred. She dipped her finger in the frosting bowl again and walked over to me, holding it out.

"Oh fuck," I groaned, my dick throbbing. I couldn't resist. What wolf could? I took her finger into my mouth and sucked it. "You taste so fucking sweet," I said.

She laughed, and I'd never seen such a pretty sight. "That wasn't me, but I'll take it." I wanted to pull her into my arms, but my pancakes needed flipping.

"Hold that thought," I begged, turning back to the stove and flipping all four of the blueberry pancakes. I turned back to her.

"Have you ever—" She broke eye contact and cleared her throat. "—been married? Or had a serious girlfriend?"

My heart picked up speed. She was definitely looking to fall in love.

I shook my head. "Never got serious—" I broke off before I said *before you*.

She was going back to school. *She was going back to school.* I had to say it over and over to remind my wolf.

Curiosity gleamed her in green eyes. "Never?"

I shook my head. "No, but I, uh, think I could be ready. Soon. To settle down." I looked away, turned off the burners and lifted the bacon onto a plate.

"What about the Green Berets?"

"Yeah," I answered. "I have to figure that part out. As I said last night, it's time to re-enlist, and of course, my superior officer and all the men beneath me are putting a shit-ton of pressure on me to stay, but I don't know. I think I might be ready to come home." I looked out the window over the sink, which had the perfect view of all of Wolf Ranch. "Especially with Boyd and Audrey starting the next generation of Wolf pups."

I slid the first four pancakes on a plate and covered it with another plate to keep them warm.

"Pups?" she laughed.

Oh shit. I quickly forced a laugh to cover my slip-up. "Babies."

"*Pups* is adorable. I just didn't expect you to get cute."

Cute. Christ. "It's, ah, an old family joke." I poured batter for four more pancakes and set the table with plates and silverware, all in the same places since I was a kid. The house had been Rob's... and mine, I figured, since our parents died, but he hadn't made many changes. He hadn't wanted to, perhaps at first because it would have been hard but later because he hadn't found his mate. I figured he didn't give a shit about things like silverware placement, but if his mate wanted things rearranged, I had no doubt he'd go for it.

Dad had made this kitchen to Mom's specs. I had no doubt Rob would bend over backward for his mate when the time came. I understood now.

Marina had already set the other two layers on top of the first and was frosting the whole thing.

"Would you work on the ranch?"

I nodded, although her back was to me. "Sure. Rob could always use the help."

"I guess once a cowboy, always a cowboy, right? Those are skills you never lose?"

"Right."

"Have you ever ridden a bull like Boyd?"

"No." I snorted. "Boyd is the only show-off

around here. The rest of us just cowboy the normal way."

She grinned at me. "What's the normal way?"

I shrugged. "Ride horses. Rope cattle. Mend fences. Throw hay bales."

"I've never ridden a horse," she admitted.

I moved and leaned against the island so she could see me while she worked. "Never?"

She bit her lip and looked up from her work. "Nope."

Jackpot. This was something I could do with her. *Without touching.* We'd be separated by horses. In the open air. I'd be able to control myself.

"Well, sweetness, you get that cake all prettied up, and we'll carry it down to the bunk house fridge. Then we'll go on a horseback ride." I leaned in, swiped a bit of frosting off the spatula and whispered, "I like knowing this will be your first time."

She paused. "I'm not sure. I have to be back to help Audrey get ready."

"Don't worry, I'll get you back in time. Besides, you're leaving soon to go back to LA for school."

Her eyes widened, and she swore under her breath.

"What's the matter?"

She shook her head. "Nothing. You just

reminded me I have to connect with my dad about the tuition. I'll send him another text."

With her mind clearly back off that random tangent, I said, "You've got to ride a horse while you're here."

She blushed, even though we'd done some pretty kinky shit and was far from innocent. "Okay."

I had no idea why taking her for a horseback ride was what I wanted to do with her. No, I did. I'd show her around the property, see what life could be like living here. With me. And we'd keep our clothes on.

"Good girl."

13

MARINA

I JOGGED down the stairs in my sneakers to meet Colton, breathless. I'd washed up and changed into a pair of jeggings so my bare thighs wouldn't stick to the saddle and threw some sunscreen on. Audrey had warned me about the high-altitude sunburns, and that was the last thing I needed in wedding photos.

I couldn't wait to go horseback riding. Actually, I couldn't wait to spend more time with Colton. Yeah, he'd made it clear he was done with the *physical* portion of our time together. I'd come right out and said it, and he hadn't contradicted me. He hadn't thrown me down on the counter to smear frosting all over my body and lick it off. But I would swear he'd wanted to. I'd thought women were the ones to give mixed signals. He'd pulled back, that was obvious, but the way he looked at me...

I didn't know what to think.

It had taken a while to finish all the decorative flowers on the cake, but Colton had chatted with me, but mostly sat quietly while I worked. Just watching. Again, the whole *looking* thing. I wasn't sure if he was naturally patient, or it was a skill honed after years in the military. Either way, I liked that the silence had been comfortable between us. I just liked his presence.

It wasn't that I'd never been the subject of male attention before. I had. Boys in high school. The engineering guys. Even some cute cowboys at the bar the night before. But I knew better than to get attached because guys left.

My father left... or never came around. The guy from college had ditched me for my lab partner. Colton was leaving. I knew it. He hadn't fed me lies to get in my pants. I'd been the one to be sneaky. I'd gotten into *his* pants under false pretenses.

I shouldn't be upset. I wasn't. Okay, I was, but I couldn't be at him. He'd done nothing wrong. In fact, he'd done exactly what I expected and maybe that was what hurt. I thought he was... more. Different. He was giving me everything I needed. Attention, devotion, ravenous affection, consideration. I had no idea I craved all of that, but now that I had it, I wasn't going to be able to go back to less.

Except I couldn't rely on him. Not for the long run. I'd leave and keep an eye out for a man who wanted to stick. With me.

Colton fit the profile of a real man more than any of them in the past. Only he wasn't some trumped up fantasy to use with my vibrator. He was right here, very much in the flesh, and I'd thought he'd returned my interest. He did, but in a hands off, no sex sort of way.

Fine. We'd ride horses. There was no way I could jump him if he were sitting on a different horse, right?

When I arrived downstairs, he held my cake on the platter, examining it from every angle. "This truly is a work of art, Marina. Did you work in a bakery or something?"

The pale pink and white flowers daintily circled the base of each layer, then spread like a garland up one side. At the top, two larger flowers were the centerpiece. It did look nice. A tad rustic without the smooth fondant often seen on some wedding cakes, but Audrey's wedding was in a barn. I thought it matched well, and so did Colton.

I shrugged, but I felt my cheeks heat from his praise. My girlfriends always raved about the cakes I made for their birthdays, but this was the first wedding cake I'd done. Somehow, Colton's words meant more to me than anyone else's. Besides Audrey's, since this cake was for her and Boyd.

"Nope. I'm self-taught. I've always loved to bake."

He studied it for another moment, rotating it in a circle, so he could see it from all sides. "It really is a talent. Let's get it in the fridge before it melts or slides off the plate or something."

He carried the cake with as much or more care and reverence as I would out of the house and down the drive. I walked beside him, opening doors, so he didn't have to do anything but carry the cake. God, if it dropped now...

Once we'd safely stowed the cake in the bunkhouse refrigerator—and told Johnny and the other guys not to touch it or deal with Audrey— Colton took me out to the stables and introduced me to a pretty pinto mare. "This is Lucy. She's a doll. She'll be perfect for you."

I knew nothing about stables, but I guessed this one held twenty or so horses based on the number of stall doors. The space was long with open doors on both ends to let in the natural light and fresh air. While the pungent scent of horses was unmistakable, the space was clean and clearly well-maintained.

I came up to the animal's nose, and I had no idea how I was going to get on top of her. "Oh, she's beautiful. May I pet her?" I looked to Colton who was watching me. He nodded and gave me a smile. He set his hand on her flank first, stroked her soft coat.

"Sure." Colton took my hand and placed it on her neck. "Nice and easy, like this. Are you nervous?"

"No," I lied. I was, but I didn't want to be. "Horses are so big. And she's watching me."

"She knows a pretty girl when she sees one."

The mare shifted and chuffed, and I tried to tug my hand away, but Colton held it in place.

"She won't hurt you, but she can pick up on your nerves. The truth is, horses are telepathic. She hasn't seen me in years, but she's comfortable because I'm letting her know I'm in charge here. I'm in control, and she doesn't have to be afraid. I don't hide my energy from her, or who I am."

I looked up at Colton. "Like with me," I murmured.

His dark gaze held mine, dropped to my lips. "That's right. I'm in charge."

A ripple of energy ran between us, but the sexual charge was laced with pain for me because he'd backed off. We weren't having sex any more, apparently. I wanted to dare him, to say, *show me, Sergeant Major*. Maybe tease him into using one of those riding crops on me or something kinky, but I'd lost my nerve with him.

Instead, I returned to his earlier statement. "Do you think I'm hiding?"

"It's hard to explain. You have to sort of let Lucy feel your energy. Try this. Tell her telepathically that you're going to ride her, and you love her."

It surprised me to hear Mr. Military Cowboy talking about energy, but I loved it. I followed his guidance and closed my eyes to project my thoughts to the horse. She whinnied, and when I opened my eyes, she nuzzled me. "It worked!" I exclaimed.

Colton grinned at me as he opened the stall door and fit a muzzle on Lucy. "See? You're a natural."

"But I'm not in charge of her. I think she might be in charge of me," I said.

"Nah, she knows what's up. Don't worry, little girl. I'll be here. We'll make a cowgirl out of you yet."

A cowgirl. I liked that. I pictured myself riding on a horse in braids and a cowgirl hat like Leigh from last night, and it made me smile. I looked down at my sneakers. "I think I need to start with some boots."

"Sure, sweetness. You ride Lucy and show me how you can be a good cowgirl, I'll get you the boots."

Okay, maybe he was still into me. I couldn't be misinterpreting his attention, could I? Or the way he looked at my body? With heat smoldering behind those dark brown eyes.

He was probably into me but didn't want to get too deep in this thing, since we were both leaving at the end of the week. I understood. I'd worried about the same thing.

I beamed at him because I had no idea how much I wanted a pair of dang boots. Or how much I like the way Colton was smiling at me. And we had our clothes on.

Despite the mixed signals from my military cowboy, Montana was soothing to my body and soul.

Not just Colton, but this place. It was nothing like LA. When I pictured myself staying here, my whole body hummed with possibility. Kind of like some people pictured themselves on a beach to relax. Or by a waterfall.

For me, it was this. The open range. The broad blue sky. The majestic mountains. I felt like I was... home.

Add to that my very own military cowboy riding beside me—even though I was silly to think he was mine—and it was perfection.

I watched as Colton put a saddle on Lucy and led her outside, then readied a big brown mare with a black mane for himself. "This is Cinnamon. She's got a little more spirit in her than Lucy, but she's been well-trained."

"Who trains the horses?" I asked as Colton beckoned me over to the fence and helped me climb it.

"Rob and all of the ranch hands. You met Johnny, Levi and Clint. Now Boyd, since he quit the rodeo. We breed horses here. Tame wild ones, too."

"So it's a horse ranch?" I felt stupid for not even knowing how the ranch made money.

"We have cattle, too." He pointed to the fields in the distance where I saw black cows dotting the landscape. We've got bulls we stud and sell free-range beef."

I noted that he still said, "we," even though he hadn't been here in a dozen years. That boded well for him moving back.

"The ranch is huge."

"Sure is. Been in the family for generations."

I studied him. "You're proud of it."

He frowned. "Damn straight."

"Then why do you stay away so long? I mean, you could work here with your brothers, right?"

He nodded as he held my hand to steady me as I swung a leg over Lucy, then adjusted my stirrups and handed me the reins.

"It wasn't the right time," he said, then helped me onto Lucy.

But now it might be? Why was I rooting for that outcome? Did I have a horse in this race? No. He'd never said what we were, but it was clear now it had just been a little fun. No one just quit the military, certainly not for me. I'd heard of people being AWOL. He had to go back. There were procedures, surely. Our time was limited, but it was hard to think that on a pretty day as I was about to go for a horseback ride with the hottest guy on the planet.

Yes. I wanted him to leave the military and

settle here because unlike the east coast, I would be sure to see him again. I'd visit Audrey for Christmas and soon after, have to visit my new niece or nephew.

Or maybe...

Maybe he'd give me a different reason to visit.

No. God, it felt dangerous to even entertain that thought. I was falling hard for this guy, the guy who'd kissed me on the forehead and pushed me into a separate bedroom the night before. That screamed *I'm done.*

Maybe he'd decided I was too young after all. I wracked my brain, trying to think if I'd done anything particularly immature last night. I hadn't been too tipsy at the bar. Or made a college-girl scene. But he'd been hands-off before we went out. I'd gotten the disgruntled vibe from him during dinner.

I patted Lucy's neck, more for my comfort than hers.

I was getting my hopes up about us turning into a long-term thing. It was totally foolish and unrealistic. I had a year left of school, and long distance relationships were difficult at best. I knew because I'd watched my freshman roommate try to navigate one with her high school sweetheart. It had fallen apart about six months into the game. And it hadn't been pretty.

Colton wasn't an eighteen-year-old college freshman. He was thirty and a Green Beret. He'd head back to North Carolina and forget about me and our fling. He was already putting distance between us now. And once he left, I couldn't compete with other women, especially with *out of sight, out of mind.*

Colton mounted his mare with far more grace than I would expect from a guy his size, and he clicked his tongue, urging both our horses forward. "You okay, sweetness?" he asked, adjusting his hat low on his head to block the sun. With that, he was an official cowboy. Panty melting.

When my horse lurched into motion, I squealed. I'd think about leaving later. Right now, I wanted to just have some fun.

"Never been better!" I called out as I held the reins and let Lucy take me wherever it was we were going. And it was true. Colton was beside me. I was trusting him in this just like everything else since we first met. I liked it. No, I loved it, and him, too. Despite my attempts to keep it from engaging, my heart was already soaring above us, basking in the warm fingers of the sun and the morning breeze. The smell of earth and grass and leather. Glowing with pleasure at the delicious male attention that kept coming my way.

Colton was going to get a crick in his neck if he kept looking over his shoulder at me, but I wouldn't change it for the world. Because every time he looked at me with such indulgence, such fondness, I melted a little more.

14

COLTON

I TOOK Marina out into the open fields and showed her how to take Lucy into a gallop. She whooped and laughed with the joy of it, her face shining with life. She was so fucking beautiful with her blonde hair bouncing off her shoulders, her eyes alight. And that smile. Fuck, it made my wolf happy, and it hit me square in the heart.

I'd had women, appreciated even more, but her smile ruined me. All that and on the back of a horse like the cowgirl-in-training she was. I was a goner because she took to it like a natural. I was surprised when anyone hadn't ridden a horse before, but I'd pretty much grown up on one. Watching her though, made it better for me. I was sharing something of myself, something I loved, without any words.

Not just the riding—the land. It was the best way to see it, on the back of a horse. I took her closer to the mountains, followed a stream for a bit, but the views... fuck, I'd forgotten how pretty it was here. Peaceful. Quiet. I didn't realize how much I missed it until I was back.

In the past, I'd been fine driving away once leave was over. I never thought twice about heading back to base. But now, with hindsight and all, I had to wonder why I was so eager for a deployment, for living in a sandbox with the enemy for months when I had this. Sure, I was proud to serve my country, but had that been the reason I'd enlisted in the first place? Had I been eighteen and eager to get the fuck out of Montana?

Yes.

I wasn't eighteen anymore.

I stopped when we crossed over onto Old Man Shefield's place. The view was to the east side of the valley. Pretty as a picture.

I leaned on the pommel and pointed. "This is our neighbor's ranch, but he died this past year."

She looked my way. "Oh. Is it okay that we're over here?"

"Of course. We were close with Shefield. We've been looking after his place for him since he broke a hip a few years back, and he had to go stay in Billings."

"Who owns it now?"

"Well, according to Rob, some niece of his inherited the place, but she hasn't been around yet to claim it. It's no matter because we'll look after the property for her."

Well, my brothers would. But I was already starting to think of myself as living here again. Staying. Getting involved in the daily operations. I had to figure out where my little niche would be. Maybe I'd settle into one of the smaller cabins in the hills just like Boyd had. I looked to Marina, wondering if she'd like that. Montana in the winter was for the hardy and a cabin almost off the grid wasn't for the weak.

She was strong, and I sure as fuck would keep her warm.

"Isn't there some hot spring and waterfall here?" Marina asked.

"You know about that?"

"Audrey told me Boyd took her there. Sounded like fun. A secret spot." She sighed.

"Of course, he did." I chuckled. It was the perfect place to take a date. In high school, we used to sneak over there at night with girls from the pack. Never when the moon was full, though. We knew better than to fuck around with raging hormones, she-wolves and the full moon. It was a good way to mark a female who wasn't your mate, and then you'd be saddled with her for the rest of your life.

The full moon was tonight, and in the broad daylight, I could feel the madness creeping in once again. My mind was filled with animalistic visions of tugging Marina off her horse and onto the ground. Settling her beneath me in the soft grass, fucking her mercilessly while I bared my teeth, ready for the mating bite. Came deep in her pussy as she screamed her pleasure, only to mark her neck for the world to see.

Fuck. I might not make it through the full moon without losing my shit.

I wouldn't be able to go back to base like this, especially after she went back to LA. I'd have to retire. I couldn't live with moon madness and stay in the military. It was too dangerous. *I* would be too dangerous. If I remained here on the ranch, at least the others would understand. I could shift. Run. Survive.

Maybe if I could keep up with her when she was back in LA, it would keep me from going insane. It was long distance or... death. Which meant we needed to get to know each other better. Out of bed. She'd quizzed me this morning about my life. I needed to do the same. I trotted my horse beside hers.

"So what kind of engineer are you? I never asked."

"Mechanical." She shrugged, looking down at her hands holding the reins. "It's boring. Math and physics. Calculations. That kind of thing."

"You don't like it?"

"Honestly?" She glanced my way, sighed. "No."

"So why study it?"

"My dad is an engineer. Math and science were always things I was good at in school. So, it seemed logical. He pretty much said if I studied engineering, he'd pay for college. I needed his help with tuition, so that's what I did."

"And you and Audrey share the same dad?"

"From what we can gather, my dad and her mom got together for a one-night stand. They were eighteen or nineteen. My dad probably forgot her name that night. He met my mom and married her a few years later. They divorced because he found a newer model in his office. He isn't much of a commitment type. Not for a wife or a kid."

"Was he glad you went into engineering?"

She shrugged. "I don't think he really cared. I mean, he pays the tuition. But I thought... I thought we'd have something in common." Looking my way, she gave me a fake smile. "Silly, right?"

I moved my horse a little closer to hers, so our legs bumped. "Nah. Parents are supposed to give out love unconditionally. It doesn't sound like your dad was even around. Nothing wrong with wanting to be closer to him."

"Well, it didn't pan out." Vulnerability flickered on her normally bright face, and my chest tightened for her.

Dammit, I wanted to make up for every wound she'd ever received. I wasn't going to push the fact that her dad sounded like an asshole. If he hadn't been there for her at all, he didn't need to ruin our ride.

"Not every man will let you down." Fuck, I'd always be there for her. Unconditionally. Even if it killed me. Even if it meant pushing her away. That made no fucking sense to anyone but me.

She shot a glance at me through her lashes, then looked away, like she didn't know how to take that. Fuck, I'd confused the hell out of her.

I'd confused the hell out of myself.

Trying to woo a female without touching her? It was like some kind of Olympian challenge.

But I was going to keep at it.

"If you hadn't chosen for him, what would you have picked as a major?"

She shook her head. "I don't know. Nothing ever called to me."

"Okay, so forget school." There was a boulder in the way, and I steered us around it. "If you could do or be anything—you know, like if you had the magic wand or genie in the bottle who could just make it come true—what would you do?"

Her eyes lit up. "I'd own a cute little small-town bakery and make people happy with my chocolate chip banana bread or my Tiramisu roll cake." She gave a sad laugh. "My dad would consider that a huge failure."

Small town. She said small town. That boded well. As for a huge failure, Marina could *never* be one. I doubted she'd believe the words, so I'd have to show her. Get her to believe in other ways.

"I want to be made happy with your banana bread, little girl."

She turned up the dial on those dimples. "I will make you some, then." She lowered her lashes. "I could make you happy in other ways, too."

She was fishing, trying to get me to say something like I wanted to drag her to the grass and fuck her here and now. Or lean toward her and kiss her. Something.

But I couldn't, and I watched her face as the realization that I wasn't going to do anything sank in.

"Come on, I'll show you the waterfall. I don't think we have time to go for a dip today, though. I promised to get you back for the wedding preparations, and I'm not going to be the asshole who breaks a promise to you."

"Wow," she murmured, rubbing her lips together.

"Wow, what?"

"The things you say."

I cocked my head. "What about them?"

She blushed. "Nothing. Nevermind."

"Come on. I'll, uh, show you the falls."

She looked away. Fuck. Were those tears in her eyes? Great. I was trying to do the right thing here, and it came across as being a total dick.

I kicked Cinnamon into a canter. I was not out here to fuck my mate. I was not out here to fuck my mate. I was not...

I took her up to the top of the ridge where the hot spring originated, and we could look down on the swimming hole.

"Wow, this is amazing," she murmured. Hopefully this place would distract her from her disappointment. Our horses side-stepped next to each other, and Lucy lowered her head to eat the tender shoots of grass.

"Can we come back? Maybe tomorrow?"

"Um... sure."

The idea of skinny dipping with her, getting her naked and wet and beneath me was going to fill my head all day. Like my wolf wasn't already in enough of a frenzy.

We headed back down the ridge, and that's when I saw it—a herd of cattle grazing on Sheffield's lower forty.

They didn't look like our cattle, these were a different shade of brown, but I urged Cinnamon forward to take a look. When we reached them, I held up my hand. "Stay here for a minute. I want to check the brand on these cows."

She reined in Lucy, and I got close enough

to one.

"JM" was the brand on its hide. Jett Markle. He was the flashy New Yorker who'd bought up the property on the other side of Sheffield's place, Rob had told me. Boyd had had a run in or two with him. Hated his guts. I could see why now. Who the fuck let their cattle roam on someone else's land? A total dick, that's who.

Rob had told me he'd shot one of our pack members last month—a teenager running in wolf form for an illicit visit to his girlfriend. Markle hadn't seen the kid shift, and I heard Boyd had given him a black eye and told him he'd shot our dog.

Not only that, Markle wanted to buy the Shefield land, perhaps double the size of his property, which meant we'd be next door neighbors to the asshole. It didn't bode well for our need to run in wolf form. The man was a fucking problem.

And now, apparently, he was moving his cows onto Sheffield's place as if he owned the place.

"What is it?" Marina asked, when I returned.

I shook my head. "They belong to the next ranch over. I don't know what they're doing on this land."

"Probably the same thing we are." She smiled impishly. "Maybe they want to go skinny-dipping, too."

My cock went hard again, and I had to adjust myself. "Stop talking about being naked, little girl."

"Or what?" she challenged with a smirk.

I growled. "Or... fuck." I looked away.

"Right." Disappointment rang in her defeated tone. "What's the scoop with the cows? Are they lost?"

"No, I have a feeling Jett Markle is using this property like he owns it."

"Well, aren't we?" she asked. "I mean, the waterfall is on the same property."

"Technically," I grudgingly agreed. "We've had a long-standing arrangement with the guy ever since my parents ran the ranch. Hell, before me and my brothers were born. He gave us permission to be here. We helped each other out. That's what neighbors do. Markle just moved his cows right on in." I sighed. "We'll have to call his niece and make sure she knows about Jett's cattle being over here."

Marina nodded. She knew nothing about cows or grazing land, so it was a short conversation. But I'd need to have a long one with Rob and what the fuck he was going to do with Jett Markle.

"Well, little girl, I'd better get you back, so you can get all dolled up for the wedding. While you're doing that, I've got to talk to Rob."

15

Marina

"So what's with you and Colton?" Audrey asked, an hour later.

After the riding, Colton had given me directions, and I'd driven one of the ranch trucks to Audrey's and Boyd's cabin in the woods. He'd wanted to drive me, but since he still had to rub down the horses, I put my foot down. In return, he refused to allow me to take my tiny rental, saying it would probably bottom out on the dirt road to get there. Once I parked in front of Audrey's and Boyd's cute place, I had to agree he was probably right.

This place was remote, and the access road was... rustic.

When Audrey came out onto the porch to meet me, I knew she was happy here. I felt a pang of jealousy... again, but tamped it down. She deserved a good man, and Boyd was it.

"Now that I finally have you all alone, I want to hear *all* about you and Colton."

She led me inside. The walls were log, the main room a living room, kitchen and dining room combination. The kitchen had been updated or was in the process of it, but I could see modern touches in the granite counters and new fridge. The rock fireplace went from floor to ceiling, and I knew it would make the place cozy in the winter.

Now, all the windows were open to let in the gentle breeze. It smelled like pine and... wildness.

"We met by chance in front of a washed-out road."

"And you shared a motel room because of the storm."

"Right."

"Yet he seemed *really* surprised when he came into the kitchen when he arrived."

I blushed. "That's because I didn't tell him who I was."

She pushed her glasses up. She'd already showered, and her hair was blown out but hadn't been styled. "But you knew who he was?"

I nodded.

"Oh boy. No wonder he was so... wild."

I thought about how he'd carried me off and punished me.

"Yeah," I said on a breathy sigh.

"Please say you used protection," she said, looking her down her nose at me.

"Audrey!" I gasped. "I'm not a patient of yours. I'm your sister."

"Even more reason to check in." When I only frowned at her, she continued with her hands up. "I'm not saying he's got chlamydia or something, but you don't want any babies right now."

"Okay, *Dr. Wolf*. I'm good. I'm covered. No STD. No baby."

She studied me, then whispered all dreamily, "I've never heard anyone call me by my married name before."

"Well, speaking of not using protection." I eyed her still flat belly. "It's a little late now to have second thoughts about that name."

She shook her head and set her hand at the base of her neck. "Zero second thoughts." She paused, smiled at me. "You like him. Colton." She studied me, and I had to look away. "I mean, *really* like him."

"What's not to like?" I admitted. "Can I shower? I smell like horse."

"Horse?"

"Colton took me for a ride." I smiled. It had been so much fun, and Lucy was a sweetheart. I was going to sneak her carrots or whatever treats horses ate.

She pursed her lips trying not to smile. "I'm sure he did," she said, leading me into the bedroom.

"Not that kind of a ride."

I set my things down. She grabbed a towel for me in the linen closet, and I went into the bathroom and turned on the shower. I stalled under the hot water thinking of Colton. He was a hot, dominant, and extremely *confusing* man. I honestly had no idea where I stood with him.

He wasn't just being nice entertaining the little sister. I'd swear he had feelings for me.

Not every man will let you down.

I wanted to give him the chance to prove it, but he wasn't biting.

When I dried off, Audrey shouted, "There's a robe behind the door."

I wrapped the towel around my head and put on the robe then joined her in the bedroom. She was putting on her makeup standing in front of her dresser with a large mirror over it.

"Your cell rang," she said her head tipped back as she put mascara on.

I dug it out of my purse and listened.

"Hello, this is Janine Fitz in the bursar's office calling again. I do need a call back about your payment for fall semester. I spoke with Mr. Thompson, and he indicated he is no longer paying the bill. Please call me right away to get this matter settled."

I stared at my phone as I ended the recording. *No longer paying the bill?* That couldn't be right.

"What's wrong?"

"Dad told the school he's not paying my tuition anymore."

She turned around, leaned against the dresser. "What? Is this normal behavior?"

I looked up at her. My stomach clenched. "Not paying? No, he's paid. It's the only parental duty he's come through on." I realized what I said and went over to her, took her arms in mine. "I'm sorry. I know he gave you absolutely nothing."

"Marina," she said, her voice soft. She didn't look upset, but she was a doctor. She had to hide her emotions for patients all the time, I was sure. There had to be a class in hiding emotions in medical school. "I don't care about him. He was never there for me. Ever. There was no void because he was never there to begin with."

She stepped away, grabbed the mascara brush and shoved it into the base, then pulled it back out. "Today's my wedding day. My dad's not walking me down the aisle. I'm glad because I only want people who truly care to be here. To me, he was a sperm donor. I'm just sorry for what he's done to you. He's hurt you."

I bit my lip, tears welling in my eyes. "Yeah, I guess I always wanted more from him, you know?"

She nodded. "Call him. Maybe there was a mix up. Maybe she got it wrong."

I swiped my phone, did as she said, even though I knew in my heart there was no mistake. "Dad, hi."

"Marina. Hello."

He didn't say anything else. No *how are you* or *what have you been up to?*

"Listen, Dad, did you get my texts?"

"Yes."

I frowned. Then why hadn't he responded? "The school called and said you haven't paid the fall tuition."

"Right, about that. I'm in Miami right now with

Cindy. We're about to get on a connecting flight to the Bahamas."

"Okay." I had no idea who Cindy was, but I assumed one of his long line of women he dated for a few months, then dumped. "So the school bill?"

"There is no money for tuition. I've spent it on a rental property in the Caribbean. We're staying there for a few months."

I stared at Audrey's bedroom wall processing his words. No tuition.

Of course, he let me down again. Every. Fucking. Time.

"But Dad, you said you'd pay for my education if I studied engineering. That's what I'm doing."

"I know, but the money is gone, cupcake."

What. The. Fuck?

"It wouldn't have been gone if you'd given it to the school."

"Things change, kid. Cindy needed a break, and I used the money."

Things change. He was right. They did. Including me. My dad had let me down. Big time. Why was I so surprised? Why did I always come last to him? Mom had gotten the shaft years ago, but I'd been strung along. Or maybe I'd just let him.

"Yeah, I've figured it all out," I snapped. "You

don't give a shit, do you, Dad? You never have." I spun in a circle.

"Okay, Marina. That's enough."

I glanced at Audrey who stood there, watching. Listening. She knew exactly what was happening.

"No, Dad. It's not enough. It's never been enough."

With that, I hung up.

Audrey came over and wrapped me in her arms. "You okay?"

I nodded, staring blindly at the bed. "I'm done. My whole life I've been trying to be the good little girl in hopes I'd keep his attention. But now I finally see. *I'm* not the problem here. That man is incapable of being a decent father. He's the definition of emotionally unavailable. He's selfish and a total dick. I think I'm starting to see what you've been saying all long. You were the lucky one. He didn't even try with you, so you didn't develop these fucked up feelings of not being good enough."

"Yes," Audrey murmured.

"All this time, I've been wondering what I could do differently to be enough for him. I was bending and contorting myself to be what I thought he wanted. I stapled, folded and crunched myself to fit into the mold I thought he wanted for me. When in fact, he never wanted me in any mold because I don't think he ever wanted kids at all!"

Aubrey blew out her breath. "I'm sorry."

"No, it's good. I finally realized it's not my fault." I tossed my phone on her bed. "None of it is. And I'm done trying to make someone love me who doesn't. The toxic cycle ends here."

"You're absolutely right." She took the towel off my head and stroked my damp hair. "You're worth more. You deserve all the love and respect in the world."

I looked her in the eye. "I don't need that asshole."

"You don't. You have me. We're family now."

I had Audrey. And I had myself. Maybe for the first time. I squeezed her tight. "I love having a sister. You're the best gift I could've ever received." My eyes grew damp. "And I love that you've got Boyd, that you're having a baby. I can't wait to be an aunt!"

"You've been the gift in my life, too."

"We don't need him."

"We never did." She set her hand on my shoulder and met my gaze. "You're strong all on your own."

I nodded. "Yes. I think I'm just realizing that."

Audrey smiled. "And you've got me. After

tonight, I'll be a Wolf, and you'll have a family here. With all of us. That is, if you want."

I moved and sat on the edge of her bed. "Well, it doesn't look like I'm going back to school."

She crossed her arms over her chest. "Oh yes, you are. You're getting that degree."

I threw my arms in the hair. "How? I don't have the money for the tuition. Even if I picked up a full-time job on the side, I doubt it would cover all my expenses. God, I'm so naive, setting myself to be like this. I should've known and been prepared."

"I have the money. I'll give it to you. You're not dropping out because our father is an asshole."

I laughed at that, completely unused to her swearing.

"School's important," she continued. "I know you don't love your field of study, but you could always switch majors."

I held up my hand. "Oh no. I'm not switching now and adding an extra year on. Besides, I don't know what I would switch to. It would be a waste of money to—"

"School is *not* a waste of money. It's good to have a degree, even if you don't go into that field for work. You can be whatever you want, Marina. You always could. Now you get to decide. You could transfer and go to school here in Montana. Or do an online program. I'm sure Colton would want you to be nearby."

A little jab of pain ran through me at that. "Colton? He's going back to North Carolina."

She tilted her head. "Is he?"

"Well, he's not sticking around for me."

She frowned. "He didn't say he wanted you to stay?" She was watching me closely.

"Definitely not. We didn't even hook up last night." Despite the fact that I'd chalked this up as a fling from the beginning, that fact hurt more than I expected. "He hasn't touched me since yesterday. I don't know, I guess the fling is over. He's made it quite clear where he stands now."

She frowned. "Um, Marina, he carried you upstairs to his room. We could all hear." She blushed hotly, even though it was me who'd had sex, not her. "I don't think he's lost interest."

"He has. That... yesterday, well, it was punishment for what I did at the motel room. He was mad at me. The fact that I knew who he was and didn't tell."

"Didn't sound like punishment to me." Her mouth tipped, and her eyes were alight with amusement.

"He got even, in a good way. A very good way. But that was it. Nothing's happened since. At least, not sexually."

Her eyebrows winged up at that. "What? Seriously? That can't be possible."

"It's possible. Trust me."

She bit her lip and was lost in thought. "There's no way he could be like this. Not with tonight and all."

"What, the wedding?" I shrugged.

She didn't say anything for more than a minute. "Give him time."

I rolled my eyes. "I'm leaving. He's leaving. The United States army doesn't have late slips, I'm sure."

"There's more there, I'm sure of it." She put her glasses back on.

"Well, I can't expect him to want a relationship after knowing each other for two days. That's crazy." Even if we did seem to fit in every way possible. And our chemistry was off the charts.

"We'll see." That was all she said, and I wondered what she was leaving out.

16

Colton

"Are you fucking kidding me?" Boyd said, running his hand through his hair and pacing.

We were in the stable, and I'd just finished brushing down Lucy. She whinnied at his loud voice. It was cool inside, but the tempers were hot. Mine included. I was glad Marina was with Audrey and would miss this convo. It wasn't going to be pretty, and I wasn't going to be able to explain the shifter-related issues and why Markle was a pain in our ass. After Marina had driven off, I'd texted Boyd and Rob that there was trouble with Markle. They'd met me here to figure out what we were going to do next.

"Nope. They were grazing all the way up by the waterfall," I told him, explaining what Marina and I had seen on our ride. I hadn't met Markle nor had to deal with his shitty ways, so I wasn't as hot under the collar as Boyd. Still, it had messed with my time with Marina and that made me hate the guy.

Rob leaned against the wall, crossed his ankles. "If they're grazing that far, it means they've been on the other property for a few days."

I agreed. They weren't fast moving animals, and there was plenty of grazeland between the opened fence and the waterfall.

"I'm going to go over and give him another black eye." Boyd turned to stalk out of the stable.

"Now hold on," Rob called. "You're getting married in—" He looked at his watch. "—three hours. I can handle Jett Markle but not a pissed off bride because her mate decided to go off half-cocked before the ceremony."

He sighed, and I watched his shoulders slump, then he turned on his heel and faced us.

"Fine. You two go." Boyd came over, took the lead for Lucy from me. "I'll get her settled and fed."

I looked to Rob, who nodded. I set the curry

comb back on the shelf, then led Cinnamon outside to wait for him to get his horse ready.

It took us less time than it took me and Marina earlier. We rode harder to get to the furthest spot from the opened fence. While I liked my brother, Rob was a silent fucker and wasn't remotely as cute as Marina. He wasn't in the mood to chat, and I wasn't going to rile him. Not that he was easily riled.

We herded the cattle back through the opening with whistling and weaving the horses from side to side to get the animals in the right direction. Fortunately, there were only about twenty or so. It took another fifteen minutes to put the fence back in place, then another stretch to ride down to Markle's house.

I hadn't been on this land since I was a kid. I remembered the family that used to live here back then. There were a couple kids who were older than us, in high school when we'd been playing in the woods for fun. They'd moved away when the kids had grown, then Rob said someone else had owned it for a few years before selling it to Markle. The house had once been white, but now it was a deep rust color. The roof was now black metal. The windows had all been replaced with sleek glass and black trim. He'd even bumped out the back for a sunroom, one whole wall was windows that faced the mountain. It had been an expensive remodel, and it looked like a fancy ski lodge. I had no idea what his heating bill was in the winter, but Markle had to have deep pockets just to pay it.

Off to the side was a brand new four stall garage that matched the styling of the house. I didn't know how many vehicles one man needed, and I was in the military and drove everything from a Jeep to a tank.

"Back here, gentlemen."

We turned at the words and steered our horses to the back. Markle was in an Adirondack chair with a plate of cheese and grapes on the glass coffee table in front of him. He held a glass of red wine.

At three in the afternoon.

Jesus.

I did a quick assessment of the enemy. Expensive clothes made to look casual. Tanned skin that came from a tanning bed somewhere in his house. Hair had product in it. His gaze was pleasant, but he gave off a vibe of being an ass.

"Wolf," Markle said by way of greeting.

We were about twenty feet from the edge of the deck, remaining in our saddles.

"My brother, Colton," Rob offered in reply

without looking my way. If Markle wasn't smart enough to figure out he was referring to me, then he wasn't going to explain.

Markle looked to me. "Another brother. How many are there?"

I stayed silent, let Rob handle this. I didn't know what had been said before, and he was the alpha. His land, his pack, was being affected by Markle, and it was his responsibility. Oh, I'd have his back, but I'd be beta in this.

"Saw some of your cows on the Shefield property. They seem to have gotten through a section of fence. Colton and I were courteous and brought them back for you."

"Oh?"

"You mentioned having some issues with wolves, so it'd probably be best for your stock if they stayed on your land."

"Didn't realize you owned the property next door," he said, taking a sip of his wine.

"Didn't realize you did either."

Markle's jaw clenched, but he didn't show any other sign of being pissed.

"The land's not yours, Markle. Stay off it," Rob said, leaning down and setting his forearm on the pommel.

"It will be."

Rob didn't stoop to reply to that, only turned his horse around and cantered away. I gave Markle one long look, knowing he was going to be a pain in our ass for the long haul.

Now wasn't the time to deal with him.

Halfway back to the ranch, I said, "The niece better get up here, otherwise the next time we see Markle, he might be in Shefield's house with his wine and cheese."

Rob gave a little growl in response.

"Your leave's almost up." He looked my way. "I'll deal with it. Boyd's here now to help."

He might as well have just shot me in the back. "You're an asshole sometimes."

"Only sometimes?" He looked my way. The corner of his mouth tipped up.

"I'm not re-upping. I'm coming home. For good."

He tugged on his reins, stopped his horse. "You're serious."

I nodded. I hadn't said it aloud, but it felt good. It felt right. Coming back here was supposed to be a week-long trip for Boyd's wedding. Nothing more. Instead, it had been a life changer.

I found Marina. I realized Wolf Ranch was where

I belonged. It was time to come home. It was time to make a life here.

"I'll get Marina here. Eventually," I said, hoping my wolf didn't lose it in the meantime.

He slowly shook his head. "Boyd's whipped. You're whipped."

"I'm fucking screwed," I countered. "You'll find your mate in time. Before the madness hits. And you'll be able to claim her, unlike me."

The wind kicked up, and I looked to the sky. Clouds were rolling in from the west, the typical late afternoon storm. After being caught in the crazy one the other night, I had to hope this just blew on through. I didn't want it to fuck with the wedding.

"I'm not so sure," he admitted. "I don't know how much longer I can hold out."

I thought of how I felt when the full moon pulled on me this last year. Riding me. Nipping at my heels every run. Every shift. Threatening to strip me of my humanity until only my wolf existed. And then there would be no more shifts. I always wanted to strip down and run. And run. But there was no relief. I found it now, not in the wilderness, but in Marina. Buried deep in her body. Her scent surrounding me. And I couldn't go there again.

I could only imagine what Rob was feeling,

being two years older. If he succumbs to this creeping affliction his human would be lost. He would never be able to shift back from human form, and we'd have to put him down.

"You will. You're alpha." As if that explained it all.

He looked to me, tipped his hat back, so I could see his eyes. "Think you'll make it with your mate halfway across the country?"

He didn't know who his mate was. I knew mine but couldn't have her.

"We're fucked, aren't we?"

"After the wedding, we'll shift and run. Okay?" It was the best way to stay away from Marina on a full moon.

All he could do was nod. "It'll be good to have you back. We'd better hurry though, or Boyd will have us by the balls for being late to his wedding."

17

Colton

THE BARN WAS TRANSFORMED. I didn't know how they did it—some female magic trick of making something special with the most basic of ingredients. Like Marina's cakes. Fairy lights were strung from the rafters, and an archway was covered in tulle and flowers. Maybe it wasn't only female magic because Levi and Clint had been in and out of the barn all day. They'd wrangled the Barn Cats, aptly named for a barn wedding, and their fiddles to play for us, although it wasn't hard to twist their arms. They loved any reason to play, and this was a good one.

Everyone was spiffed up, even me as we stood at a makeshift altar waiting for Audrey. I hadn't brought any uniforms home with me, so I was in my crispest jeans and shirts with a bolo tie. I'd buffed my boots, but a shine on my shoes was normal for me. We were inside the barn, the doors wide open to let in the natural light.

It had been a while since the last shifter mating celebration, but that had been different. This time, there were human wedding traditions, like the bride walking down a center aisle. There were only a few chairs as the guest list was small. Becky, Leigh and Anna were here, but Audrey hadn't invited any other human friends. The rest of the guests were shifters from the ranch or who lived up in the hills.

Rob stood in the center. As alpha, he would conduct the service. While Boyd had already claimed Audrey, this was a legal wedding in the eyes of the state. Rob was a Justice of the Peace and could officiate. He'd had the role for years, ensuring the pack members had the legal perks of being claimed as well as the shifter ones.

The fiddles started, softly and without the raucous punch I was used to from the duo.

I stood beside Boyd—who was as calm as a fucking cucumber—and watched as Marina walked toward me, a bouquet of wildflowers in her hands. The wind had picked up even more, and her hair swirled around her face.

My breath caught in my throat at the sight of her. She was wearing a simple dress, the color of spring grass. It was made of a soft, gauzy material that floated and wisped about her. It fell to her knees and she wore cowgirl boots on her feet. I wasn't sure if Audrey had gifted her the pair or if they were borrowed, but she looked like a little slice of Montana heaven.

"Fuck," I whispered, watching as she moved to stand on the other side of Rob.

He leaned toward me. "Am I winning the fifty bucks?"

I looked at Rob, saw the grin and growled.

Then Boyd looked toward the open barn doors, and his mouth dropped open. There was Audrey, pretty as could be, but I couldn't look away from Marina. My wolf wanted to cut across the ten feet that separated us and tell Rob to make her mine, legally, then I'd toss her over my shoulder, take her somewhere private and claim her. But I couldn't. Not only because Boyd would kill me and bury me in the back forty, but also because Marina didn't even know I was a shifter. Didn't even know how much I fucking needed her.

Hell, maybe I didn't either, until now. Until the ride this morning. Until it wasn't just a craving of my wolf. It was my heart that was telling me to make her mine.

I loved her. How the fuck that happened in two short days, I had no idea, but it wasn't going to change. I had no idea what to do now. It wasn't just my wolf that needed sating. I needed it too. I needed Marina.

Audrey cut into my view, and I blinked.

Boyd met her, took her hand and leaned down and whispered something in her ear. She smiled up at him, and he pushed her glasses up her nose. She wore a white dress with a similar gauzy material as a top layer. It had little flowers embroidered on it. Her dark hair was pulled back in the front but lay over her bare shoulders. I had no idea if she ever wore contacts, but she had on her glasses. Boyd had told me she was the picture of a sexy doctor, and I had to agree. She looked beautiful, in love and not the least bit nervous.

Maybe it was because she was already claimed, and this was just a human formality. A celebration, really. Yet it felt more to me. Doubly official.

They turned to face Rob, and he smiled at them. A full-on fucking smile.

I hadn't noticed it all that much before, but the older he got, the more he looked like our dad. His bearing was that of an alpha. His voice, as he spoke of love and a permanent bond, was full of authority. He was made to be a leader although we all wished he'd have been able to wait a few years.

Our parents would have loved this. Loved Audrey, the baby she was carrying. And Marina.

"You may kiss the bride."

Boyd leaned down and kissed Audrey while everyone clapped and cheered. I'd missed the entire ceremony, lost in my thoughts. Hell, I'd turned sentimental. A romantic. Next, I would need a hanky to wipe my tears.

But I wanted this with Marina. To profess my love for her. Completely and honestly in front of everyone we cared about. There were no secrets between Audrey and Boyd. I wanted that with Marina, but it couldn't happen. Not now. Fuck me, I was screwed.

The first clap of thunder made everyone cheer, like it was the pistol-shot starting off the celebrations.

In true wolf-pack fashion, the place instantly

transformed to a party. The Barn Cats struck up their instruments before the chairs were even moved to the sides. I pushed my way to Marina's side, drawn like a magnet.

"Hey, beautiful." I swept her up into my arms and twirled her around. Her scent flooded all my senses. It must have been the full moon because I could swear it made me drunk. The room suddenly spun even though I'd stopped moving. When I looked down at Marina, her eyes widened.

"What?"

"Your eyes look strange in the light—almost gold."

Shit.

I should tell her what I am. She was my mate, she needed to know. Then again, if I weren't taking this to the next level yet, I'd be breaking pack law. And right now, I was fucking surrounded by pack members all looking on with curiosity.

I'd made my decision to give her the life she deserved. The alpha had agreed.

"Hey, Colton. Looks like Boyd's not the only one who found his—" Shelby, one of our younger pack females, stopped talking when I gave a tiny shake of my head. "—found himself a woman," she said after a slight hesitation.

Dammit. This was getting downright awkward. I really needed to tell Marina, whether the rest of the pack approved or not. Or Rob. What kind of mate was I keeping such a crucial secret?

Honestly, when I first learned from Boyd that his mate was human, I'd been surprised the pack had accepted her without much fuss. I'd expected to hear some snide comments or whispers tonight, but I hadn't. Maybe it was because the alpha was on board with it. Maybe it was because Boyd would probably rip anyone's head off who spoke bad about his mate, no matter her DNA.

Their acceptance though, gave me hope. Would they be fine with both human sisters as mated into the pack?

"Shelby, this is Marina, Audrey's younger sister," I said, settling my hand at the small of Marina's back. I wouldn't stop touching her.

Shelby studied Marina with curiosity. "Sister, huh? Interesting. Well, this whole town loves Audrey. She's everyone's favorite doctor."

Marina smiled. "Yeah, she's pretty killer, isn't she?"

If she thought there was anything weird about the conversation. She didn't let on.

"Come here, sweetness, I need to tell you something about me." I hoisted her legs up around my waist. I fucking loved carrying her. The wild, riotous cravings I had being near her calmed when I had all of her in my arms. Like my wolf knew I had her. She was safe. Mine.

Thunder boomed again and the rain came on, hard. Like suddenly the faucet in the sky got turned on full-blast. Just like the other night. It was storm season in Montana, but hell, they were strong. It pounded the barn roof, which unfortunately wasn't completely water-tight.

I heard squeals and laughter as people had to move to avoid getting wet. The Barn Cats stopped and moved to a dry spot, then started back up. Boyd pulled Audrey close and spun her away from a drip. They were happy, completely unfazed by the change in weather. Thank fuck, they wouldn't let a little rain ruin their night.

Marina laughed and squeezed her thighs around my waist, her arms looped around my neck. I found a quiet corner and sat down, arranging her on my lap, facing me. "What did you want to tell me?"

I glanced around. My wolf was tearing at the surface, but I shoved him down. Yeah, she had to know. She had to understand why I was pushing her away. Why I couldn't kiss her. Couldn't fuck her like I wanted. She deserved to know because keeping it from her was wrong. She'd be mine, no doubt of that. Later, sure, but I wanted her to know everything now. No secrets. "You see all these people here?"

"Yes."

"They're not just ranchers, they're all sh—"

A whistle pierced the air and Rob's alpha voice carried over the rain and music. "Everybody, listen up."

The Barn Cats stopped playing.

"I hate to break up a party, but I have no doubt the creek along the canyon road back into town is rising pretty fast. Might even flood."

There was complete silence as everyone remembered what had happened to our parents in a storm just like this one.

"We don't mess around with that," he added, for those who didn't know our sad history. "Don't want you all in danger or stuck here all night. So, anyone who needs to get back into town better leave now!"

"Oh my gosh," Marina exclaimed, scrambling down from my arms.

"Hang on, little girl," I said, but it was too late. Becky, Anna and Leigh came over to say goodbye. It was a parade of flurried greetings, and then Marina wanted to send them with slices of cake since they'd miss all of the food.

"There's no time, sweetness. They need to get out of here now, or it could get dangerous driving home," I warned.

She stared at me wide-eyed, then her look softened. Yeah, Audrey had told her. "Okay."

"Save me some for later!" Becky said, squeezing Audrey then Marina for another quick hug before the ladies and half the shifter crew ran out into the pouring rain.

There were about ten of us left along with the band, who didn't seem to mind being stuck here overnight. They'd crash in the bunk house. They played a tune I'd heard at Cody's the night before. Audrey and Boyd moved into the middle of the space and started to line dance. I had no idea Boyd knew the steps. Neither did anyone else because they were clapping and whistling, impressed.

I had to admit, my brother was smooth.

Marina and a few others joined them. Marina crooked her finger at me to participate, but the one thing I didn't do was dance. No fucking way. Besides, I was having too much fun watching. The camaraderie of the Wolf pack made me think back to times before our parents died.

Yeah, I was coming home. It was time. And all because of the pretty blonde doing the Boot Scootin' Boogie.

A horrible crack filled the air, so loud I watched Marina jump. Immediately after, a huge crash sounded, then part of the barn roof caved in and fell all around us.

Automatically, I ducked down but glanced up, watched the wood as it fell. A tree branch came with it. There was a huge cottonwood behind the barn, and it must've been struck by lightning.

On instinct, I ran and tackled Marina to the floor, covering her body with my own, my arms cradled around her head to keep anything from hitting it. All around screams, growls and snarls rang over the crashing wood and pelting rain as pack members' wolves sprang to the surface to help them survive.

It was only through years of military training I suppressed my own urge to shift. It helped that I had Marina safely beneath me. If I hadn't, my wolf would've gone nuts to save her.

"No!" a woman screamed. The terror in her voice made me jerk my head up. She was throwing slats of wood away with shifter strength. *"Liam?"*

A child. Fuck, a kid was under there.

I scrambled up to help her. Boyd and Rob were

right there, too, throwing the pieces of wood away until we uncovered the fallen boy, a shifter child no more than ten years old.

"Don't move him!" Audrey yelled, pushing her way through and dropping to her knees beside him, forgetting she was wearing her pretty wedding dress. Rain poured through the destroyed roof. "His neck may be broken."

"Don't worry, it'll heal," Boyd said to her in a low voice. He squatted beside her, dripping wet. "It would heal faster if he was old enough to shift, though."

Audrey knelt beside the boy, carefully checking his pulse without moving him. "He's alive." She looked to the boy's mother and nodded in reassurance.

"*Shift.*" Rob's voice rang out with alpha command. Every shifter in that barn felt it, and the familiar internal response.

Some of the younger wolves—teens or more submissive pack members, actually shifted, even though Rob wasn't talking to them. Whimpers sounded over the rain as clothing ripped and shredded and the animals were released.

Marina gasped, grabbing my hand and stepping closer to me. I wrapped my arm around her and pulled her snugly against my side.

"He doesn't shift yet," the boy's mother cried.

"*Shift*," Rob moved to stand directly over the boy, blocking some of the rain and commanded again.

"He can't." The boy's mother wept. "Don't you think he would've if he could?" She appealed to Audrey. "Is there anything you can do for him, Doctor?"

Marina trembled at my side, her slender body shaking with the trauma of everything she'd seen.

Fuck. She saw. She knew. There would be no coaxing her to the truth. It had hit her on the head like a piece of falling roof. I hadn't wanted her to find out this way. Fuck.

"*Shift, Liam!*" Rob commanded again. Marina looked up at me in confusion, but I didn't say anything. This time he infused so much command it exploded through the barn. My body shuddered in response. More pack members shifted, whimpering and tucking their tails. "*Shift now.*"

It worked.

The boy's body moved of its own accord, joints snapping and rearranging, clothing tearing until he lay on his side, a panting young wolf.

Audrey stroked her hands down the wolf's spine, like she was checking for breaks. There had been no bleeding when he was in boy form, so I had to assume he'd been hit on the head from falling debris.

"Now isn't that a sight? Liam's got black fur, Mama," Boyd said calmly, looking up at the boy's mom from where he knelt beside Audrey. "Give him a little bit. He'll be okay now." While he wasn't a doctor, he assured the weeping mother. "I snapped my neck more than a few times riding bulls and pulled through just fine."

"Oh, thank you," the mother exclaimed, dropping down on the other side of her shifted son. Clarinda, I think her name was. I remembered her from high school.

Rob took charge. "Everybody out of the barn. Clearly, it's not safe. If you can get home, go on. If not, we'll put you up in the bunkhouse for the night. Johnny, Levi, pick up Liam and carry him to a bunk so he can recover."

Everyone moved at once, Johnny and Levi doing as told, Clarinda following them out into the rain. Audrey and Boyd stood. He set his hands on her shoulders as he spoke to her. She nodded and then was pulled into his arms.

Boyd looked to Rob. "If you don't need us, we're leaving. I want to get to the cabin before that small stream between here and there rises. The last place I want to be on my wedding night is with you guys."

"What if someone else is hurt?" Audrey asked.

Boyd tipped her chin up, wiped the rain from her face. "Everyone's fine. You and the baby are on my watch. It's time to get you home. The only one who can't shift and heal is Marina." They looked our way. "And I'm sure Colton will take good care of her."

I squeezed Marina close, but I didn't have to say a word. There was no fucking way anything was going to happen to my mate. I'd had a moment of sheer terror when she wasn't by my side when the roof collapsed. It only confirmed my plans. I was staying. She was it. I just had to wait it out. Hell, maybe I'd even go to LA to be with her. Whatever the plan was, she was in it. Front and center.

Audrey's glasses were speckled with water, and her face was marred with concern. She didn't care that her dress was wet and muddy or that her hair was dripping wet or that the party was ruined. She was thinking about others like a true member of the pack.

Rob nodded. "Go."

Boyd didn't waste a second, steering Audrey out into the storm and to their wedding night at their cabin in the hills.

Only Rob, Marina and I remained in the barn. Rob looked to me and nodded again, giving me silent permission to tell her. Although, that fucking cat was out of the bag.

I turned to Marina and cupped her face. Beneath my skin, my cells vibrated with the need to claim her, but I forced the sensations down. "Remember, yesterday, you surprised me in the kitchen?"

She looked up at me from her tucked spot against my chest. "Yeah."

I wiped her wet hair back from her face. Just like I had that first night. "I've got one of my own. Surprise. I'm a shifter."

18

Marina

I'M A SHIFTER.

No, not just a shifter. A *wolf*.

They all were wolves.

Colton was part wolf.

WOLF!

Holy shit.

I felt like I was trapped in a *Twilight Zone* episode.

Audrey hadn't been surprised.

She knew.

Of course, she knew. Her husband was part wolf.

That meant she knew Colton was part wolf, a shifter, and didn't tell me.

I was going to *kill* her.

Yet, her knowing and being okay with it enough to marry one of them—and have his baby—was the one thing that kept me from totally freaking out. Like, if she'd already accepted it, I could, too. Right?

I saw a boy, unconscious, turn into a wolf. Like a transition in a movie. Could Colton do that? Could *all* of them?

"Surprise? This was what you were going to tell me before... " I pointed up.

It must have reminded him where we were, for he led me out of the damaged barn and tugged me beneath one of the overhangs, so we were out of the rain.

It was just like the other night when we met, standing in a downpour together. Now, we knew so much more about each other. Things I'd never, *ever,* imagined.

His brows dipped in concern. "Yes. Are you hurt?" He had a strong arm wrapped around me, but my knees wobbled so much from the adrenaline, I still feared I might collapse onto the ground. He wiped rain from my face, as if the rain might hide some kind of wound. Sniffed.

Oh God, now I knew why. He could *smell* me. I didn't know what it meant exactly, but it was so obvious now.

"No."

"I have to ask for your vow never to tell an outsider about us," he said, his breathing ragged. We were both riled from the tree falling through the roof, but this was more. He was back to being intense, just like when we'd first met. "It's extremely important, for the safety of the pack."

I flipped through my mental notes on werewolves, and what I came up with scared the crap out of me.

"Is Audrey one now, too?"

His mouth dropped open as he stared at me. "No."

Thunder rumbled in the distance.

"Are you going to bite me and turn me into a werewolf?" What did it mean that the thought excited me as much as it scared me? Strangely, I was already willing to jump into any adventure with Colton by my side. Even a plunge in the paranormal pool. Yet, he'd made it pretty clear he wasn't interested.

"What? No. Oh, Christ. Don't believe what you've seen in the movies. It's not a disease passed through biting. We're a different species."

I shivered, absorbing that information. I had no idea about species or... wolves. Maybe I should have been a biology major.

"It's not safe here. I've got to get you inside where it's safe and dry." Colton swung me up into his arms as if I weighed nothing and ran for the main house.

"Colton!" I cried.

"I won't keep my mate in danger." He said it almost as a vow.

Mate? What did that mean to a wolf? A shiver ran through me that had nothing to do with the rain. It was something about the way he'd uttered those words. Rain pelted down on us, instantly soaking us through. I clung to his strong shoulders, marveling at how wonderful it felt to be so heroically cared for.

Two days. I'd known this man for two days. It already seemed like so long ago.

He didn't stop once we got inside, just carried me up the back staircase to his bedroom, sat me on my feet just like he had yesterday morning after he'd found me in the kitchen.

And then he tore off my wet dress. *Tore* it, as if it were made of tissue. The sodden material opened, then he slid it down my arms and let it fall to the floor.

He stared at my naked body—well, I was wearing skimpy panties and nothing else—and his eyes changed to amber, and this time I recognized it for what it was. *His wolf.*

Did it mean he was excited?

It must.

A low growl rose in his throat. "Fuck, Marina. You're impossible to look at. I shouldn't have brought you in here."

I reached for his wet shirt, undoing the button, unsure if I should be flattered or upset. "Why not?"

He caught my wrists and threw me up against the wall, my hands pinned beside my face. His mouth was on me before I could finish gasping, claiming me with a searing kiss.

"Fuck, Marina," he repeated, dragging his open mouth down the column of my neck.

"I thought... I thought you didn't want me anymore."

"I do. Fuck, I can't control myself around you." He licked the rain from my skin, sucked on it until I knew he'd leave a mark.

"You did last night. Why didn't you... why did I

not stay with you if you want me? I, oh God, I don't get it." I squirmed against him, trying to rub, to feel more. His hold was firm. I wasn't going anywhere, and the idea of that made me so hot.

He pressed his wet body against mine, his leg insinuating between my thighs, giving me something to grind down on when he pinched my nipple.

"Colton," I moaned. I'd missed this. One night without him, and I was lost.

"I need that pussy," he growled. He sounded half-crazed, but I loved it. He hoisted me higher on the wall, until my hips were the height of his head, then he tossed my legs over his broad shoulders and cupped my ass. "No more panties."

He literally ripped them off me. The fabric tore, digging into my skin a little before they gave way and rent in two. And then his mouth was on my core. A hot tongue on cool flesh. He lashed me in long strokes, licking and sucking. He nipped my labia, grazed my clit with his teeth.

Oh, this was so intense. He was as frantic for me as I was for him. I writhed and moaned, wrapping my arms around his head, both terrified and thrilled with my precarious position and the intensity of his passion.

It was so much, all at once. I got dizzy from the sensations flooding through me. The pleasure, the build-up, the emotional ride of being Colton's on-again off-again sex interest.

Finding out they are all shifters.

I ground my core against his face shamelessly, seeking the release I so desperately needed. I'd never gone from zero to orgasm so fast before. Ever. I'd been primed for him ever since I fell asleep beside him the day before.

Just as I got close, though, Colton lifted his mouth from my core. He looked up at me with a look I'd never seen before. So fierce. So wild. Primitive.

"Wait, no," I whimpered. "Don't stop. Please."

The only sound from Colton was an unearthly growl. He carried me to the bed and tossed me down, and I bounced. Before I even settled, he was climbing over me. His eyes glowed pure amber. His lips were wet from my core, the tendons in his neck were taut. The humanity was completely gone from his face.

A shiver of fear ran through me. He liked to be in control, a little wild, but this? It was different. It was as if he'd been tightly coiled before, and now he was unleashed.

What did I really know about these Wolf brothers? Maybe he'd lied. Maybe he *was* about to turn me into a werewolf. Could I trust him?

His touch was rough as he shoved my legs wide and pulled down his zipper. When his cock sprang free, he fisted the base, stroked it from root to tip. Lifting his head, he looked at me. Prey. I swore his teeth had changed.

Oh my god—vampire fangs. No, *wolf* fangs! Either way, they were fucking long and sharp.

"Colton?" I scrambled backward on the bed, bumping into the headboard.

He grabbed my hips and dragged me back under him.

"Mine," he growled.

"Okay, fine, but I don't understand. You're... changed. *Colton?*" Alarm rang in my voice as I shoved at him.

He growled and rolled my hips over, slapping me on the ass.

"No, not like this." I turned around.

He stared down at me. I wasn't sure if it was the word *no* or what, but that somehow brought him out of this. I was all for wild and rough, but it was as if Colton hadn't been with me, as if he'd been driven by something inside him. By his wolf.

He shook his head and turned away from me,

stumbling back toward his closet, pants open, clothes wet.

"Colton?" My heart pounded.

He shook his head as if flicking water away like an animal.

"Fuck, Marina," his voice sounded choked as he looked me over. I was naked, sprawled on his bed. I no doubt had a huge hickey on my neck, red marks all over from where he'd touched me.

My pussy throbbed with need, the orgasm having been so close.

He was breathing as if he ran a race, then wiped his mouth with the back of his hand. He sniffed, and I realized he must have smelled my arousal. "I... fuck, I can't do this with you. It's not going to work."

I sat up, pulling the bedcovers up to cover myself. "What do you mean?"

He walked to the door, ripped it open, then turned to face me.

"You. Me. *Us*. I gotta go. Go back to your bedroom, Marina. You can't stay here tonight."

Oh my God. What in the fuck was happening?

Before I could even figure it out, Colton left, bolting out the door and slamming it shut behind him. I heard his heavy footfall rush down the stairs, then the slapping of the screen door off the kitchen.

What had happened? Was he disgusted by me? The smell of me on him like a poison? He'd just walked away. Left. At least he'd been very clear about it.

I dropped to a fetal position on the bed, pain exploding in my chest. I'd thought... again, I thought a guy would stay. Would want me for me. But no. Colton was perhaps the worst.

My dad had never given me crumbs of affection. I'd thought he had, but really, there had been nothing there from the start. I'd hoped there would be more, but Cindy and the Caribbean were more important than me. The guy from college who went after my lab partner? Whatever. Sure, I'd been lacking, but he hadn't offered me anything. I'd thought he had, until I met Colton.

Fuck, Colton opened me up, cracked me open for me to see who I really was. I wasn't just the along-for-the-ride girl I'd thought. I was more. I knew what love was, what a connection should be. Devotion. Obsession. Lust. All of it. And yet, I still wasn't enough. I couldn't be, or he'd be here in bed with me right now, making me scream his name.

Colton was wrong. It seemed every man would let me down. I'd been thinking I wasn't enough for them. My dad. The jerk from college. Colton. I'd thought if I was enough, they'd be in my life.

But I was enough. And I fucking deserved better than this.

COLTON

I RAN BLINDLY out of the house. Didn't even know where the fuck I was until I ran smack into Rob.

"Ready to run?" he asked, then looked me over. "Dude, why's your dick hanging out?"

Shit. I reached down, shoved myself back in my pants, although it fucking hurt. I was so hard, it was actually painful. And my balls...

There was no way I'd get the pants zipped.

"Do I owe Boyd fifty bucks?"

Panting, I glared at him. "No, nothing happened."

He arched a dark brow. "Really?"

The rain had let up while I'd been upstairs with Marina. It was barely a drizzle now, and the thunder was off to the east. The storm had blown through as fast as it had arrived.

The air was cooler. Damp. The scent of green grass and wet dirt filled my nostrils, making Marina's sweet scent disappear.

"No," I snarled. "Why do you think I'm standing out here with you?"

He knew what I was going through. How close I was to madness.

"Fuck." I ran a hand over my face, my hair still damp from earlier. "Let's run. Hard." I yanked off my clothes right there outside the back door, not bothering to stow them somewhere dry. I left them with my boots in the mud. I didn't wait for Rob and shifted, then took off.

We didn't usually run on our property. Not with neighbors around. Pack law was to keep to the mountains where we couldn't be seen, but I couldn't wait that long to shift. It was almost dark, and I didn't give a shit. If the alpha was pissed, he could deal with me later.

I felt his presence behind me, probably sticking close in case I did go mad. He might be able to keep me from losing my humanity completely by ordering me to shift back at the end of the night if I couldn't do it on my own.

And I might not. I'd never felt the madness this

strongly before. The wild beast within me taking over, scratching to be free.

Fuck!

I ran at top speed, following a path through our land that led to the mountain range beyond.

I'd scared Marina. My teeth had descended, coated with the serum that would forever mark her with my scent. I hadn't been capable of holding back.

She'd been too perfect. Her pussy had just been that sweet. Her flavor was still on my tongue. Her skin had been like wet silk, her cries of pleasure, the rough tug on my hair indication she'd been right there with me. She liked me wild, but that.... That had been something else.

I'd been something else.

I should never have risked being in a bedroom with her. Taking her clothes off. That was utterly idiotic! Why had I thought I was in control? With her, I never would be. I couldn't risk her. Ever.

Marina. *Marina.*

I had to run off this wildness, this madness, so I could get back to her. Explain everything. Take her into my arms and make amends. Tell her I'd wait for her. However long it took.

I raced up the side of the mountain, my nails

digging into the wet earth as I climbed. And when I hit the top, I sat and howled.

Boyd had been right. Fate was a whore.

If I made it through this night, I would never defy her again.

19

Marina

I couldn't stay here. Staring at the shelf of Colton's childhood trophies, I realized this was the last place I could remain. Not just his bedroom, but Wolf Ranch.

Which was... full of wolves.

Audrey and Boyd were all sequestered away in their cabin for their wedding night, and I doubted they'd come up for air tomorrow. Or the next day. They weren't planning a honeymoon, so I didn't think they'd make an appearance anytime soon.

And I sure as hell couldn't stay in this house with

Colton and Rob.

I wasn't even sure if I could trust them now that I knew what they were.

And Colton...

Colton had broken my heart.

Just like my dad. No, I'd broken my own heart over him. I shouldn't have loved him in the first place.

I sat up, wiped my face, then went across the hall to my room. Threw on some clothes. I didn't even know what I'd done to have Colton freak. I guessed I was too human for him. I didn't measure up. Same old story.

Except, no. Fuck that. I shoved my arms through a hoodie sweatshirt and pulled it over my head.

It was their loss. I wasn't the problem. I wasn't the one who wasn't good enough.

I couldn't go combing over every event, trying to figure out what I screwed up this time. How I wasn't exactly what he wanted.

I *was* enough, dammit. I was enough for me. Audrey was right. I deserved all the love in the world. Someone who wouldn't jerk me and my feelings around.

If Audrey knew what a dick Colton had been, she'd be on a warpath, but I wasn't ruining anything for her. I sat on the edge of the bed, shoved my feet into thick socks, then put on my sneakers.

Right now, I was going to take care of myself. And that meant going somewhere I felt comfortable.

Away from this house. This ranch. The nearest place I could think of was that stupid motel from a few nights ago. It was on the way to the airport. In the morning, I could get a flight out of Montana and figure out the shit show of my life.

Audrey would be there for me, I knew. Hell, she'd even offered to pay for college. But I had to figure out me. What I wanted. I'd thought it was to be an engineer and make my dad happy. That had been dumb. Here, I thought maybe I made Colton happy. Clearly not. I needed to make myself happy. And tonight, that was to get the hell out of here before Colton came back.

I saw Audrey get married. My job here was done. She was going to be in bed with Boyd for longer than I wanted to wait. They could eat the untouched wedding cake when they came up for air. I'd be doing us both a favor if I changed my flight to tomorrow morning and just made a clean break.

Yes. That was exactly what I needed to do. I shoved my things in my suitcase and zipped it shut.

It only took a few minutes before I was tripping

down the stairs, the suitcase banging against the wall as I ran. Outside, the air was cool and damp, but the rain was over, like God approved my plan. Good, that meant I should be able to get through the roads to the motel. At least I hoped it could. I hustled out to my car, tossed the bag in the back seat, started it up and took off. As I sped away down the muddy road, I saw Levi come out of the bunkhouse to look down the drive at my retreat.

Well, good. He could let them know I left.

As I made my way through the dark down the long drive and beneath the Wolf Ranch entry arch, I realized I didn't care if I ever came back.

COLTON

IT WAS LONG past midnight when I'd finally run my wolf into the ground.

Some of the ranch hands and other unmated members of the pack had joined us, needing the release on the full moon, like we had. But most had stayed home with the storm and the wedding events earlier.

All but Rob had gone home. I'd pushed too hard, too far for any of them to want to keep up. He had been nipping at my flank for hours, trying to get me to return, but he wouldn't leave me.

I ran down the mountain for the ranch house. Even exhausted, that underlying mania still there.

Mate her. Mark her. Make her mine.

The fucking full moon. No. Not. Happening.

I'd get Rob to lock me up tonight, if he had to. Even though I desperately needed to talk to Marina, to explain why I'd left, I couldn't risk getting near her. Tomorrow, I'd explain it all. Hell, grovel even.

I shifted when we got to the back door, then picked my clothing up from the mud. Jesus. It looked like a car had driven over them. I'd been so out of my mind when I ran down here, I hadn't even noticed if anyone had seen me shift.

At least all the humans had gone.

Levi walked up from the direction of the bunk house, like he'd been up waiting.

"Hey, Colton." He stood back, kept his hands in his pockets.

I ignored him, stalking into the house. If he wanted to stand there, he could check out my bare ass. "Not now."

I didn't have it in me to focus on anything but

keeping my wolf under control until morning, when I could fix things with Marina.

"She's not up there, man," he called.

I froze, a violent tremor running through my body.

I spun on my wet heel on the wood floor. *"What do you mean, she's not up there?"*

There could only be one *she* he was referring to. Marina. My mate.

"She drove away, man. Right after the rain stopped. Didn't say anything, not that I was out here. I don't know where she went."

Audrey. She'd gone to Audrey's. It made sense. She'd want to talk to her sister. I shook open my muddy jeans and tried to step into them, but Rob stopped me. "Go get some clean clothes on, Colton." His voice was low and even. Like he was trying to calm me.

"There's no time!" I snarled.

He grabbed my arm. "If you can't keep it together, I'm gonna fucking sit on you until morning. Clean up. Get your clothes on. Get your fucking head on straight." There was alpha command in his words, which took my wolf craze down a notch.

I inhaled sharply through my nostrils and

answered the only way a pack member can when his alpha pulls rank. "Yes, Alpha."

I ran upstairs, taking the steps two at a time. Marina's smell was everywhere, filling my nostrils, sending my wolf into a fucking tailspin. He was on a non-stop howl inside me, frantic to find her. The run had done nothing to soothe me.

I took a ten-second shower, only because Rob was right—I was covered in mud. I pulled on fresh clothes at the same time I ran down the stairs and grabbed the keys to my rental truck.

Please let her be at Audrey and Boyd's. Please.

Rob was saying something to me as I left, but it didn't register. All I could think about was getting to Marina.

I climbed in the truck and started it up, sliding in the mud when I gunned it too fast.

I needed to calm down, or I'd get the truck stuck. I eased off the accelerator until I was down the road, and then I gradually increased the speed.

The lights were off at Boyd's. I didn't give a shit. I climbed out and pounded my fist on his door.

I barely saw the anger on my brother's usually easy-going face when he swung the door open, buck naked. "You'd better have a really good reason for showing up on my wedding night."

Wedding night.

Fuck, I'd already forgotten.

But fuck if I'd apologize. "Where's Marina?" I boomed.

My brain was too scrambled to reason through the situation. To realize that Marina wouldn't have gone to stay with them on their wedding night. She wasn't out of her mind, like me.

Boyd's face clouded.

Audrey showed up behind him, dressed in a silky white robe. She wasn't even wearing her glasses. "What's going on?" Concern sharpened her sleepy voice.

"I'm sorry," I forced myself to say, looking down. It was one thing to see my brother naked, another to see my sister-in-law barely dressed, especially when I'd been an asshole and interrupted them. "Marina's gone, and I was wondering if she was here or if you knew where she went?"

Audrey's eyes grew wide. "What did you do to her?"

I deserved it, but her words still hit me like a punch to the gut.

Fuck.

What had I done to her?

I'd scared her, for sure. Was that why she'd ran?

I rubbed a hand over my face, trying to remember exactly what had happened. I'd been eating her against the wall, and then I'd thrown her on the bed to have sex with her. My teeth had descended. She'd been scared and tried to stop me, but it didn't get through my haze until I'd heard the word no.

Fuck!

"I lost control," I admitted. "The full moon. Fuck. I wanted to mark her. And I scared her. So, I got out of there to keep her safe. I told her—"

Oh shit.

I knew why she'd left. What had I said? Something colossally stupid. Like, *I can't do this with you.*

Had she taken it as a rejection?

My sweet, sensitive girl? She carried that insecurity from her dick of a dad. Not being good enough. Had I made her feel that way, too?

Jesus, I would cut off my own arm if I had.

I had. I knew it. And it was far worse coming from me. I was her safe place. Her person of trust. The one who let her be who she really was. I let her submit and give herself freely to me. That meant she gave everything to me. Even her heart.

And I'd been a dick. I'd destroyed her.

"You told her what?" Audrey snapped.

"Not enough," I admitted. "I didn't tell her she was my mate because—"

"You never told her she was your mate?" she practically shouted.

"I didn't want to pressure her. She's so young, and she still has school. She needs to have fun and figure out who she is, what she wants. Party. Hell, dance. I was going to try to keep my wolf in control and give her time for that."

Audrey crossed her arms over her chest as she listened.

"If she were a she-wolf, she'd know she belonged to me. But Marina's just a sweet young human who didn't know about shifters until tonight. It's not like I could just bite her. I couldn't claim her without her consent. It'd be too much to throw at a young woman who just met a guy and has no idea what a shifter even is."

Audrey put her hands on her hips, and Boyd grabbed the front of her robe and tugged the two sides together. "So, what did you say?" she asked, ignoring him.

I dropped my head and closed my eyes in misery. "Something stupid," I muttered. "But I'm going to fix it. Right now. I'm going to find her."

"You'd better," Audrey said. "And you tell her

everything. Don't make assumptions about what she can handle or not. She may be young, but she's not stupid. She can make her own choices about things. About you. She doesn't need you to protect her."

"The hell she doesn't," I grumbled, but I was already marching for the truck. I had to find Marina tonight before I lost my ever-loving mind.

"She needs the truth, Colton. That's all she's ever needed."

Those words sliced deep because they were true. So. Fucking true.

I nodded and walked away.

"You'd better fix this," Boyd called after me, and I would've flipped him off if I could spare even the slightest distraction from my purpose.

But I couldn't. I needed to get to Marina.

Where in the fuck had she gone? Where could she go at this time of night? The ride to the airport was over two hours. There weren't any more flights out at this time of night. If she were headed back to LA, which made the most sense, she'd have to wait for morning. So I'd head to Bozeman, check the hotels. I'd find her. I had to. I couldn't let her leave like this. Just like Audrey had said, she needed the truth. All of it. Because that single sexy picture of her on my phone couldn't be all I had of her.

20

Marina

I shouldn't have come to this same motel. Being here reminded me way too much of Colton. At least I'd been given a different room. After standing in the shower for forty-five minutes, hoping the hot spray of water would eventually wash away the weekend, I crawled into bed for another cry.

I'd replayed every single word we'd said to each other. Every move he made.

Dammit.

Why'd he have to be so damn perfect for me? Why did he have to be the one guy who really got under my skin? Our sexual attraction was off the charts, but it was even more than that. It was everything about him--his dominant, protective way. How he'd lifted me off that signpost in the rain and laid out my wet clothes to dry. And everything in between. He'd been so trustworthy. Attentive. Protective.

Yet the image of him crashing out of the bedroom earlier came back and made a sick lurch in my belly.

Why did he leave? What had gone wrong?

But no, I wasn't going there anymore. I wasn't ever going back to my pattern of trying to figure out what I'd done wrong or could've done differently.

This was on him.

And yet, still, the stupid scene kept replaying in my mind. And when I stopped looking for my mistakes, it shifted.

His eyes had been glowing. He'd been more wolf-like than human. As if all the time we'd been together, he'd been holding back. That was pretty scary, but hell, Colton was an intense guy with depths I'd never imagined. In that moment, I'd been afraid and told him no.

He'd stopped. Looked at me with horror, retreated. Fled.

I sat up in bed staring at nothing in the dark.

Colton was honorable. A man I trusted enough to let tie me up and do all manner of kinky things to me, even as a near-stranger.

I'd told him no, and he'd stopped, even when he was so far from being himself.

I can't do this with you. It's not going to work.

He'd been agitated. No, worse than that. Riled. Enflamed. Pushed. We'd been about to have sex, and he stopped when I told him to. I wasn't a guy, but I know it must've been hard to pull back like that. I'd seen his dick, and he'd been right there. Almost feral with the need to fuck me.

I had to stop blaming myself. A woman was allowed to say no at any time. For any reason. I'd just never expected to say no because a guy was part wolf.

Now, I could look more objectively at this situation. Maybe in that moment, when he'd looked down at me sprawled on his bed, Colton had decided it couldn't work with a human. Because I didn't understand *as a human*. Or because he'd be too rough. Too wolfish for me.

But Audrey and Boyd made it work. While she hadn't told me everything about their sex life, I knew they had sex. Knew it was hot. Knew it was kinky. She'd even told me Boyd was a little rough, and she loved it. But was he human rough or wolf rough?

Ugh. I fell back on the pillows. I *had* to stop thinking about this. I'd left Wolf Ranch physically. I needed to block it all out of my mind now, too. Move on with figuring out my life and future. Discover what I wanted.

I wanted Colton.

Dammit--no! I slapped a hand over my face to try to block out the unwelcome thoughts.

And that was when a heavy knock sounded at the door. "Marina?"

I gasped, stared at the dark door.

Colton.

My spine stiffened, my heart instantly revving into a rapid staccato. My stomach flip-flopped. He was here.

"Marina, I know you're in there, sweetness. Please let me in."

I didn't move. My whole body was a live wire, trembling with potentiality.

"Just let me try to explain about tonight," he said through the door. "Hear me out. Then if you tell me to go, I'll go. I promise."

A tear escaped one of my eyes and ran down my

cheek. I was already crying, and I didn't even know what he was going to say.

"Please, Marina. I fucked up. I failed to tell you something crucial. Something you needed to know. About us. It's important. Life or death important. I won't hurt you."

I silently slid my feet to the floor and stood. My knees were weak and shaky. Was I holding my breath?

"I was trying to protect you, Marina," he continued, as he was going to tell me everything whether I opened the door or not. "I didn't want you to get hurt. But I know you did, anyway. I was stupid. Please just open this door, sweetness. I'm having a really hard time not bashing it in to get to you."

I sob-hiccupped and covered my mouth with my hand, fresh tears flooding my eyes. I heard his growl and knew somehow, he'd heard the sound. Knew I was crying.

He did want me.

Colton Wolf wanted me. And there was an explanation for his behavior.

I dashed across the room and threw the door open.

"Thank fuck," he muttered, already entering, like his body was drawn to mine like a magnet. He wore jeans and a black t-shirt, perfectly tame, but his eyes were wild, almost desperate. For me.

I meant to be strong and proud and not need him at all, but instead I let myself fall right into his arms, and he lifted me up, held me tight. I should have made him beg. Grovel, but I just didn't understand. I was mad at him, but I needed to know why.

"Oh, thank fuck," he breathed. He wrapped me up and sank to the floor, to his knees, keeping me tight against him. "Thank fuck. I was losing my mind without you, sweetness."

"How... how did you find me?" I asked, my cheek pressed to him as I absorbed his energy, just like I had with Lucy, the horse.

"I'll always find you," he murmured, kissing the top of my head. "It also helps you have the smallest car in the state. Easy to spot."

I regained my senses and tried to push away from him. He didn't let me go, though. Instead, he began speaking in a rush. "You're my mate," he blurted. "Wolves don't choose their mates, fate does. I recognized you as mine the moment I first caught your scent out in the rain."

"Wait... what?" I pushed away from him enough to see his face. He shifted me, so I straddled his waist, and our faces were just inches apart. Was that why he'd sniffed me out in that storm? It had seemed so strange then. Now? It made sense. I'd seen Boyd do it, too, the other morning in the kitchen.

"You smell people?"

"I smell *you*. I'd know you as mine anywhere."

His gaze burned with intensity, but his eyes didn't glow amber. They were his human irises this time.

"Wolves only have one mate. Sometimes it takes a lifetime to find them. Some never do, and they go moon mad and have to be put down."

"*What?*" This was a lot to absorb all at once. Moon mad?

Colton plowed on, like he had to get all the words out. "When a male shifter finds his mate, he bites her to embed his scent in her skin, so other males know she's been claimed. I know... this is probably freaking you out," he said quickly, probably seeing the shock on my face. "That's why I didn't spring it on you sooner. Why I didn't tell you what you are to me. Tonight was the full moon, and it made me crazy. My wolf wanted to mark you. Right there in my bed even when you didn't know what it meant. I was too aggressive. Too wild. I scared you, so I had to get out of there. I had to shift and run off the urge, so I wouldn't hurt you."

He sighed, stroked my hair back. His gaze dropped to my lips, then to look me in the eye. "I'm sorry, sweetness. I thought finding you, my mate, would quell some of the moon madness that's been creeping up on me, but I don't think my wolf will be satisfied until I've fully claimed you."

"B-by biting me?" I swallowed hard. Audrey had asked if I'd used protection. Well, she might have given me a little lesson in wolf mating instead of worrying about me getting pregnant. She was in big trouble not telling me about all this.

He winced. "Only to claim you." His hand went to my neck, slid down to my shoulder, brushed his fingers delicately over the spot. "Here. Once. To know you're mine forever."

I shifted my shoulder away involuntarily.

"Don't be scared of me, little girl. I would never touch you without your permission. I wouldn't mark you without your consent. That's why I left. You said no. You're young. You're human."

He sighed, ran a hand over my hair and down my back again as if he couldn't stop touching me.

"This probably seems crazy. I know mating for life is too much to lay on you, and that's why I pushed you away. You're only twenty-one. You've got college. Friends. Fun. Hell, line dancing. I can wait until you're ready to settle down." He sighed but sounded a lot like a growl. Had that been his wolf complaining? "I'll try, anyway. I probably can't be near you during the full moon. But we can wait. Get to know each other better until you're ready. If you'll still let me try to woo you, that is." He said the words quickly, almost frantically. He'd been holding them in, and like water behind a breaking dam, it all rushed out.

Tears fell down my cheeks. It *was* a lot.

But I wasn't afraid. Not at all.

I was happy. Excited.

Colton didn't just want me. He wanted to claim me.

As his. For life.

I cupped his jaw, looked into his eyes. "When you were at the door, you said it was life or death important."

Regret washed over Colton's face, and he dropped his forehead to mine. "Nevermind about that," he said softly. "I don't want to put that on you."

My pulse picked up speed again. I lifted my head and held onto his biceps. "Put what? Is it because of the moon madness?"

His muscles flexed beneath my hands. "It's all right, sweetness. I can hold out as long as you need me to."

Oh wow. That was so hot. Brave. But one-sided.

Colton was willing to go mad before he pressured me to commit to him.

"I know you're a fighter and protect people. It's your job. But I don't want you to sacrifice like that for me. Not without me having any say. Don't you think I should decide what's best for me?"

"You're young," he countered.

"And you're an idiot. I want you. I don't have a wolf in me, but I know, just as you do. Your sacrificing yourself just because you decided what's best for me is total bull."

His mouth opened, but I put a finger over his lips. "Don't even think of punishing me for my sass. If we're in this together, like you say, then *we're in this together*. We discuss things. Like grownups. Supposedly you are one."

He nipped the tip of my finger, and I yanked it away.

"You're right," he said. His shoulders relaxed a bit, but his hold was still fierce. "I couldn't tell you about us being shifters if you weren't staying."

"All you had to do was ask me to stay," I whispered.

He shook his head. "I couldn't deny you a life."

"You're giving me one, Colton. Silly boy, it's a life with *you*."

Words weren't enough. It didn't seem like I was getting through his thick skull. I leaned forward and bit his neck, and he chuckled in surprise. His skin was warm, his taste like salt and pure Colton.

He growled, and I loved it. "Are you claiming me, little girl?"

"Yeah," I said softly, leaning back and looking in his eyes. "I think I am."

He wrapped his large palm around the back of my neck to keep me in place. "We'll do this however you want, sweetness. You can take all the time you need. Just please don't walk away from us."

I growled this time although it didn't sound very wolflike. "If I remember correctly, you walked away, not me."

He stared, then nodded.

Tears popped into my eyes again. "I'm not walking away," I promised. "I want you, Colton Wolf. I just don't like feeling jerked around."

"Fuck. I'm so sorry, Marina. I never meant to

mess with you. You're everything to me. And not just because my wolf recognized your scent. Because I fell in love with you this weekend. I met a bright young woman who loves deeply and spreads sunshine everywhere she goes. You are truly amazing. You've created as close a family-bond with a sister you only met a year ago as I have after a lifetime with my brothers. You're easy-going, smart, and fun. You're kind and so very giving--especially in bed. You make amazing cakes. I want to take the time to get to know every tiny detail about what makes you tick."

I let out a watery laugh. "You haven't tried my cakes, yet."

He grinned, his eyes roving over my face with so much affection, it warmed me to my toes. "That's right. We'll have to rectify that. Wedding cake for breakfast tomorrow?"

"That sounds great," I murmured. All the sadness, the heartache, the confusion were gone. In it, I felt light. Happy.

"So, you're giving me another chance?"

I shook my head and his face went blank. "No. I'm giving *us* a chance."

"I love the sound of that." He pulled my hips over his groin, so my center rubbed over his hard length, and then groaned. "Fuck. Now we have a problem."

"What?"

"I need to get my hands all over you, show you how satisfied I'm gonna keep you, only--" He broke off and swallowed.

I ground down on him, rubbing my breasts against his chest. "Only what?" I purred.

His breath fell hot on my neck. His fingers tightened on my hips. "Only..." He pulled my hips down hard over his erection once more. "I'm so fucked, Marina," he admitted on an exhale.

I laughed because now I knew this wasn't a rejection. It was Colton's lust for me. His inability to hold back. He wanted me *too* much. His fear of hurting me or pushing me too far too fast.

"How so, Sergeant Major?" I flicked my tongue over his earlobe.

"I-I can't hold back. And there's no fucking way I can leave you again, either."

I leaned back and caught his eye. "So don't."

He blinked, and his eyes were yellow.

"Don't hold back," I said. "I'm ready to be claimed."

He slid his hands under my pajama shorts, cupping my bare ass. "You-you can't be sure. You're too young to decide."

"Shut up." I pulled my tank top up to show him

my breasts. "You don't get to tell me I'm too young. And you don't get to decide for me. I want my wolf-bite. And I want it now."

"But school."

"I have two semesters left. I can do them anywhere. My dad's not involved anymore--long story--so I don't have to be in LA."

"Oh fates. Oh Christ. Are you saying you want to live at Wolf Ranch?"

"Are you saying you're getting out of the military?" I countered.

"I decided that earlier. With Rob. I'm getting my papers and getting out. Going home. For good." A vulnerability crossed his features. "With you?"

I beamed. "See, all you had to do was ask."

Colton had me up on the bed in seconds, my pajamas stripped from my body with a few quick tugs. "I'm gonna fuck you so hard, little girl," he growled, parting my legs.

He settled his mouth between them, licking into me like a demon.

No, like a wolf.

A crazed, moon-mad wolf about to mark his mate.

As I writhed and dug my fingers into his hair, I couldn't freaking wait.

21

Colton

THERE WAS NO STOPPING NOW. Even though my mind screamed at me to pull back, to make sure she meant it, my wolf was too hungry for her. I had to pleasure her. To hear her scream my name. To claim her as mine, forever.

It was finally fucking happening.

Holding off had been the longest 48 hours of my life.

I feasted on her like a starved man. Her little sighs, moans and cries only fueled my desire to satisfy my mate before I took my own satisfaction.

"Marina," I growled her name every time I came up for breath, to make sure her lashes still fluttered in ecstasy. Every time, she lifted her head and met my wild gaze and moaned, "Yes."

I used my tongue in every way I knew how, flicking, fluttering, penetrating. I could stay here for hours between her thighs. Her taste, her scent, were all over my face. And while she was the one to be marked tonight, I wanted to be drenched in her, so everyone would know I was claimed, too.

Yet I needed to have her come. Needed to give her the pleasure I'd denied her since yesterday and myself. It was crucial I could please her, that my naughty girl was all. Fucking. Mine.

I rimmed her anus and made her squeal. I screwed two fingers inside her, carefully at first and then when she practically ripped the sheets to shreds in her tight grip, I didn't hold back. I methodically stroked her inner wall, seeking her G-spot as I swirled my tongue around her clit.

Her cries grew more frantic, her head arched back in pleasure, mouth open. "Yes, Colton, please. Please don't stop! Please, ohmygod!"

I pumped my fingers inside her and affixed my lips over her little nubbin, suctioning onto it and pulling. She would come. Now. And again. And again.

"Oh my God," she squealed again, hips lifting off the bed and bouncing. Her tight pussy contracted around my fingers, her arousal practically dripping onto my palm. I waited until she'd finished, laying replete and panting, then crawled over the top of her and unbuttoned my jeans.

"This is crazy," she murmured in awe when she looked up at me again. "Are your wolf's eyes amber?"

I drew in measured breaths, trying to keep control and nodded. If she could see them, then my wolf was right at the surface. Ready. Waiting. I couldn't bite too deep. Couldn't hit an artery. She was human and wouldn't heal instantly like a she-wolf would.

Fuck, I'd never gotten to ask Boyd how he'd done it, but I remembered seeing where Audrey's mark was when she'd had on her wedding dress earlier.

That wasn't the only thing I had to think of to protect her. Condom.

I still needed to use a condom, no matter how badly I wanted to mark her with my seed at the same time. She was in college. Not ready for pups. She'd said as much, and I'd respect that.

I fumbled with the wrapper, my dexterity dulled with the roaring in my veins, the sweet taste of the serum coming down my fangs, meant for her skin.

She grabbed the package from me and opened it, helped me roll it on.

Oh fates. She wanted this as badly as I did. That made me fucking crazy.

I tried to hold back--I swore I did--but it was impossible. Settling my hips between her parted thighs, I lifted one of her knees, lined up and speared her with a single thrust.

She gasped, eyes flying wide, her shoulders sliding up the bed.

"Sorry, I'm sorry." I cradled behind her neck and lowered my head to kiss her. "Beautiful little human. My sweet mate. I don't want to hurt you."

She rocked up to meet me. "I'm not hurt. I'm not fragile. You were wild with me before here at the motel. In your bed at the ranch. Be wild again. Show me your stuff, wolf-man."

I gave a pained laugh. She was so fucking cute. So cute it hurt my ribs. Made pressure in my chest, like there wasn't enough room to breathe.

She reached back and braced her hands on the headboard, issuing a challenge with her eyes. *Give it to me.*

Challenge accepted. I eased out and thrust again. Her knees drew up on either side of me, an offering. It let me get deeper, and suddenly, I couldn't get enough. Her inner walls rippled around me as if trying to get me deeper. I braced my own hand on the headboard and pounded into her, holding her in place by her shoulder.

The room spun. I was too hot. Flushed with fever. Need. Desire. Lust.

Her head went back, her eyes closed, her lips parted, and her breath came out in pants. A flush crept from her cheeks, down her neck and to her breasts. The small tips wobbled as I took her.

Nothing mattered except fucking the daylights out of my little mate. Seeking that finish that both of us so desperately craved. Nothing existed but her gasps, her moans. Nothing fulfilled me like the ecstasy of her expression.

"Marina..."

"Colton!" Her voice held thready desperation. She was on the edge. Ready to plunge over the other side.

Sweat dripped down my brow. "Come for me, sweetness. Let me have it all."

It was as if she'd been waiting for me to allow her to do so because as soon as the words were uttered, she came. Because she's that fucking sweet--coming on command.

Christ, I was going to have fun teaching her all the pleasure of surrender. Showing her how an alpha wolf took care of his female. Punishing and rewarding. Coaxing out all the naughty desires she might have lurking within her. We'd only had two days. A lifetime was before us.

And then I came. Lights exploded behind my eyes. I filled the condom pumping into her. Then I pulled out and waited, breathing, breathing, waiting for my vision to clear, so I wouldn't make a mistake.

"Hold still, sweetness." I brushed her hair back from her sweaty neck. The thought of scarring her perfect skin killed me. I'd hate for her to be self-conscious about the mark, not wear those little tank tops anymore. So I dragged my lips across her shoulder and rolled her to the side to kiss down her shoulder blade. She turned her head to look up at me, to watch. And there, below the shoulder blade, in the fleshy part of muscle under her armpit, I bit.

I came again, and the condom slipped off, so I jizzed all over her ass.

Fuck...*fuck*...FUCK. It was like one of those movie clips where scenes flashed across the screen one right after the other super fast. I'd thought of this moment. Heard about it from my dad. Boyd. Knew what to expect. I'd craved it. Needed it.

But nothing, *nothing,* compared to reality. The feel of her skin beneath my tongue, the way my serum seeped into her, the taste of her flesh, her blood. The knowledge that Marina was mine forever. Fuck. The orgasm was so intense, and my dick wasn't even inside her.

I was in love with Marina. I was proud Marina was mine. I was humbled by the woman, that she gave herself to me. Me! I would spend the rest of my life trying to make her happy because nothing I could do would compare to what she just gave me.

Marina's whimper brought me back to reality in an instant. I forced my jaws to unclench and eased my teeth out of her flesh. Wiping my mouth with the back of my hand, I said, "Marina, sweetness. It's over."

I licked the wound closed. My saliva would provide antibodies to promote quick healing and prevent infection. "Tell me you're okay." I pulled a pillow case off one of the pillows and pressed it against the wound before I rolled her to her back.

Her face was a little pale, but she nodded. "Ouch."

"I'm so sorry, baby. It will never happen again. I

will never hurt you as long as I live. At least not intentionally. Or unless you like it." I winked, and she relaxed, settling back into the pillows.

"Now I'm yours?" she asked, her voice soft.

"Now you're mine."

"Forever?"

"Until death do us part. I will always provide for you. Protect you. Pleasure you. I will spend the rest of my days making up for hurting you."

"Will you… " She bit her lip.

"Say it."

"When can I see your wolf?" She looked almost shy, as if the words weren't right.

"My wolf?" I cleared my throat.

She nodded, and I smiled.

"Fuck, yeah. It's big. Bigger than a normal wolf. Do you want to see it now?"

"Yes!" She sat up and put a hand over the bite wound.

I was still on my side, so I leaned forward, kissed the spot, licked it again to get it to heal faster. It would be sore, so showing her my wolf would be a good distraction.

"Don't be scared, all right?" I looked into her eyes, searched for a depth of concern that she might freak out. She'd seen little Liam shift earlier, but seeing her man turn into a wolf for the first time could push her over the edge.

She took a deep breath, nodded.

Pushing off the bed, I stripped off my clothes, let them drop in a pile on the floor. My cock was hard again, but I ignored it, only looked at Marina as the air around me blurred, and the room filled with the sound of cracking joints.

Marina stifled a scream. I'd warned her. I was huge. And a wolf.

"Oh my God," she whispered, staring.

I jumped onto the bed, sank to my belly and lowered my head to her lap.

She held her hand out, and I licked it. "Wow," she breathed, studying me. She stroked my ears. "You're so soft." She buried her face in my fur. "You're magnificent, Colton."

I let my wolf take a moment to revel in her attention, then shifted back. With my head in her lap still, she stroked my hair. "Wow," she said again.

"Not too freaked?" I asked, moving slowly, so I settled her on the bed in my arms. We stayed like that for a while, quiet. I'd thrown so much at her, I wanted her to think, to work through everything. I'd wait for her questions, and I'd answer them all. No secrets.

When I thought she'd fallen asleep, she drew in a long shaky breath. "What now?"

"Whatever you want, Marina. Whatever is best for you."

"I don't want to go to LA" She sounded surprised, but sure. "I don't even like college. I hate engineering."

I stroked my thumb across her cheek. "I didn't want to fuck up your career path, little girl."

"You didn't. I did that--by choosing the career my dad wanted for me. I don't know--maybe I'll finish online or something, but I'm definitely not going back. I'm going wherever you go. North Carolina. Here. I don't care. I needed a fresh start but didn't realize it was with you. Hell, it *is* you."

I stopped to feel the resonance of her words. To notice how my wolf had quieted. The intensity around Marina was the same--the need to focus all my attention on her, to give to her. To protect her. But that crazy, gnawing need had diminished. In its place was warmth. And something else--something I hadn't experienced before.

What was it?

Fuck. It was contentment.
I was Marina's fresh start.
And she was mine.
It was fucking perfect.

EPILOGUE

MARINA

We walked in the back door of the main house the next day. *Late.* It had been close to two in the morning when Colton found me at the motel and even later when I'd fallen asleep. No, I hadn't fallen asleep. I'd passed out from too many orgasms. We didn't stir until after eleven when housekeeping knocked on the door. While the motel was like a little sex cocoon for us, we didn't need to stay any longer. Reality was A-OK with me.

The bite on my side didn't hurt, but I could feel it. When I'd put my fingers to it, turning to the side and lifting my arm up in the bathroom mirror, I'd seen the wound was closing. I'd grinned at the mark because I knew it wouldn't disappear. They would be small scars from Colton's teeth.

It didn't scare me. It thrilled me. For the rest of my life, I'd have his mark to remember what we'd just shared, that it would last forever.

Colton drove us back to the ranch in his big truck. He said he didn't give a shit about the rental, that the company could come pick it up for all the good the thing could do in Montana. I wasn't going to argue because I agreed. They needed to give it back to the circus where they'd found it. Secretly, I thought he didn't want me out of his sight, or away from the ability to touch me. Again, I wasn't going to argue. I didn't want to stop touching him either.

So when the screen door slapped shut behind us, we froze and stared, hand in hand. Sitting at the large kitchen table was... everyone. Rob, Levi, Johnny, Clint and the other ranch hands whose names I couldn't remember. Boyd and Audrey were there too. In the middle of the table was the wedding cake, half decimated. Everyone had empty plates-- coated with a few crumbs and dabs of frosting on them--and mugs of coffee.

We stared. They stared back.

Then Rob began to clap. All eyes turned to him, but when Colton pulled me into his side, and I looked up and saw his grin. So did everyone else. They clapped, too.

Boyd stood, came around the table and slapped Colton on the back. "Way to go, brother."

"Oh, my God, are they clapping because you... because we--"

Colton looked down at me. Winked. "They don't need to see the mark to know I claimed you." He sniffed, blatantly, and I caught on.

Mortified that everyone was aware we'd had sex, and I'd been bitten by a shifter, I buried my face in his chest, face hot.

"Welcome to the family, Marina," Rob said. I lifted my head, and he was right there before me. I had to tilt my head back to meet his gaze, and I thought I saw the corner of his mouth tip up in a smile. He reached out, stroked my hair in a brotherly way, which made Colton growl until Rob went back to his seat.

I hadn't ever seen Colton this relaxed, this... happy, even while doing his possessive growling. It was because of me, of us, of the bite. He didn't have to worry about moon madness any longer, and we'd laid it all out. There was nothing between us now. And, apparently, I smelled like him.

I tugged on his shirt, and he leaned down. "If I smell like you, then does that mean you smell like me?" I whispered.

He grinned. "Abso-fucking-lutely. They'll know I've been used and used well."

My mouth fell open, and I swatted his rock hard abs.

He laughed, and I stomped over to the empty chair beside Audrey. "I want some cake," I announced.

Clint picked up the large knife and sliced me off a chunk, placing it on a clean plate. He passed it around to me, and Johnny handed me a napkin and fork.

"Coffee?" Levi asked, rising and going over to the pot.

"Please," I said.

I watched as Colton dropped into a seat across from me and was given a slice of cake as well. His eyes were on me as he took his first bite.

"The cake's incredible," Audrey said, wrapping her arm around my shoulders.

"I'm sorry the reception was ruined." I looked to her, saw she was relaxed and smiling, just like

Colton had been. That meant her wedding night had been a good one.

"I'm glad Colton found you. He came by looking for you. We were really worried."

I glanced at Colton, but he didn't say a word. He hadn't told me he'd bothered Audrey and Boyd after I'd left. "He did."

"I don't have to ask if everything's okay."

I couldn't help but smile. "Everything's fine."

Audrey made a show of sniffing the air. "Oh yeah, I definitely smell him on you," she teased with a big smile. "Just kidding. My nose doesn't work like that."

I rolled my eyes. "God, what is it with all of you and sniffing?"

Glancing around the table, all the guys smiled, but didn't look the least put out.

"I knew you'd been with Colton the second you showed up the other day," Boyd said. "It surprised me because he hadn't shown up yet, and you two weren't supposed to know each other."

I put a hand to my face. "Well, I guess I smell like him permanently now, so it's not like you'll be able to know every time we have sex."

There, I said it.

"Oh, they'll know," Colton added. "Because I

won't be able to stop smiling." He grinned, and my heart melted.

"Do you need me to look at your bite?" Audrey asked. "I should probably dress the wound."

I shook my head. "No, it's good," I whispered, then shoved cake in my mouth. The lemon flavor was just right, and the sponge was moist. The frosting cut the tang, and I was pleased.

"You're both here to stay?" Rob asked, taking a swig of his coffee.

Colton looked to me. "I've got papers to deal with. Some red tape. But yeah."

"I'm going to finish school. Somewhere," I added, so they all knew I didn't plan to spend the next year in LA.

Colton nodded. "We'll get here. Soon."

"Good." That was the extent of Rob's enthusiasm about our moving to the ranch, but I was used to him being cool with his emotions. "We've got a barn to repair."

I set my fork down. "I can help with that. The barn's old so it wasn't made with pre-fab trusses. I can work with the contractors to ensure the roof not only meets code but can withstand a hurricane."

Rob looked to me, studied me quietly, but I could tell he was thinking. "There aren't any hurricanes in

Montana, but it would be best to rebuild as sturdy as possible. We'll be sure to include you when we start the rebuild."

I glanced at Colton, and he gave me a small nod. Maybe my engineering knowledge could be beneficial. I didn't want to make a career of it, but it felt good to be useful.

"This cake is delicious, Marina. Can you bake me one for my birthday next month?" Johnny asked.

Colton growled, but Johnny was undeterred.

"Sure. What's your favorite kind?"

"Chocolate."

"My favorite," Audrey said. "Clint, cut me another piece." She pushed her plate into the center of the table.

"Why didn't you tell me that's your favorite? I wouldn't have made lemon poppy seed."

Audrey looked at me and rolled her eyes. "*Every* flavor is my favorite. And since I'm eating for two, I get a double helping. Forget engineering, *bake*."

No one argued with the pregnant woman. Clint pushed the plate back toward her with a huge chunk from the bottom tier. She turned to look at Boyd, fork raised as he dared to argue.

He held up his hands. "Whatever my girls want."

I tugged on her arm to make her turn my way. "*Girls?* You know you're having a girl?"

Audrey shook her head and shoved a piece of cake in her mouth. "No. Way too early to tell," she said as she chewed. "He thinks we are."

"We are," Boyd replied, adamant.

Colton chuckled as he took a sip of his coffee. Boyd glared at him, then pointed. "You wait, brother. Your turn's coming."

Colton looked my way, and I got a little lost in his dark gaze. "Can't wait."

I'd made it clear I wasn't ready for kids, but the way he stared at me and the way my body tingled in response, and the idea of carrying his baby, made me think sooner than later.

"Also, I can't wait to try your famous chocolate chip banana bread."

"I'll make some for you today," I promised.

"Boyd got a text this morning from Shefield's niece," Rob said, changing the subject. Boyd nodded. "Natalie Shefield. She's coming out."

"Not to sell the place?" Colton asked.

"No," Rob said grimly. "To live. By herself."

"Why do you sound disgruntled about that?" I asked, confused. I knew nothing about the niece who inherited the ranch next door other than what

Colton had told me, but I knew she'd be in the middle of a mess with Jett Markle and the entire Wolf family. The way Colton had spoken about Mr. Shefield, I knew they'd watch out for her.

Rob just shook his head. "I don't like the idea of a single woman living down there by herself. She sounds young. Probably pretty. I just see trouble, especially with Markle."

I managed not to roll my eyes over the *probably pretty* part. "Well, you all will look after her, I'm sure."

"Yeah." Rob scrubbed a hand across his face and stood from the table. And then I thought he muttered, "That's the trouble."

I shot a glance at Colton, but he just shrugged. I had to hope Rob would warm up to her... or anyone. Only time would tell. In the meantime, Colton and I had some planning to do. About the rest of our lives.

He winked, as if he could read my mind.

I couldn't wait.

Ready for more Wolf Ranch?
Get Wolf Ranch: Feral next!

Pack Rule #3: The alpha must mate.

The stronger the alpha, the greater the danger.
Moon madness could claim me any time now.
I've looked all over the continent, gone to mating games, but I still haven't found the she-wolf meant to be my mine. I've already become too feral in bed. I'm not safe—not for random females. Especially not the human variety.
One just moved into the ranch next door. She's way too tempting. And I'm way too dangerous.
I have to stay away. I don't dare get near her.
Because I would die before I ever let anything harm the little human.
Including me.

Get Wolf Ranch: Feral!

MARINA'S RECIPE

Marina's Famous Chocolate Chip Banana Bread
(For a delicious gluten free version, substitute rice flour for the flour)

½ cup butter (softened)
1 cup sugar
2 eggs
3 mashed ripe bananas
1 cup flour
1 tsp baking soda
½ tsp salt
½ cup chocolate chips

Cream butter and sugar in a mixer. Add eggs and bananas. In a separate bowl, sift together (or mix) flour with baking soda and salt. Mix in gently to banana mixture. Stir in chocolate chips. Pour in a loaf pan and bake at 350 for one hour.

NOTE FROM VANESSA & RENEE

Guess what? We've got some bonus content for you with Colton and Marina. Yup, there's more!

Click here to read!

GET A FREE VANESSA VALE BOOK!

Join my mailing list to be the first to know of new releases, free books, special prices and other author giveaways.

http://freeromanceread.com

WANT FREE RENEE ROSE BOOKS?

Go to http://subscribepage.com/alphastemp to sign up for Renee Rose's newsletter and receive a free copy of *Alpha's Temptation, Theirs to Protect, Owned by the Marine, Theirs to Punish, The Alpha's Punishment, Disobedience at the Dressmaker's* and *Her Billionaire Boss*. In addition to the free stories, you will also get bonus epilogues, special pricing, exclusive previews and news of new releases.

ALSO BY VANESSA VALE

For the most up-to-date listing of my books:

vanessavalebooks.com

On A Manhunt

Man Hunt

Man Candy

Man Cave

The Billion Heirs

Scarred

Flawed

Broken

Alpha Mountain

Hero

Rebel

Warrior

Billionaire Ranch

North

South

East

West

Bachelor Auction

Teach Me The Ropes

Hand Me The Reins

Back In The Saddle

Wolf Ranch

Rough

Wild

Feral

Savage

Fierce

Ruthless

Two Marks

Untamed

Tempted

Desired

Enticed

More Than A Cowboy

Strong & Steady

Rough & Ready

Wild Mountain Men

Mountain Darkness

Mountain Delights

Mountain Desire

Mountain Danger

Grade-A Beefcakes

Sir Loin of Beef

T-Bone

Tri-Tip

Porterhouse

Skirt Steak

Small Town Romance

Montana Fire

Montana Ice

Montana Heat

Montana Wild

Montana Mine

Steele Ranch

Spurred

Wrangled

Tangled

Hitched

Lassoed

Bridgewater County

Ride Me Dirty

Claim Me Hard

Take Me Fast

Hold Me Close

Make Me Yours

Kiss Me Crazy

Mail Order Bride of Slate Springs

A Wanton Woman

A Wild Woman

A Wicked Woman

Bridgewater Ménage

Their Runaway Bride

Their Kidnapped Bride

Their Wayward Bride

Their Captivated Bride

Their Treasured Bride

Their Christmas Bride

Their Reluctant Bride

Their Stolen Bride

Their Brazen Bride

Their Rebellious Bride

Their Reckless Bride

Bridgewater Brides World

Lenox Ranch Cowboys

Cowboys & Kisses

Spurs & Satin

Reins & Ribbons

Brands & Bows

Lassos & Lace

Montana Men

The Lawman

The Cowboy

The Outlaw

Standalones

Relentless

All Mine & Mine To Take

Bride Pact

Rough Love

Twice As Delicious

Flirting With The Law

Mistletoe Marriage

Man Candy - A Coloring Book

OTHER TITLES BY RENEE ROSE

Made Men Series

Don't Tease Me

Don't Tempt Me

Don't Make Me

Chicago Bratva

"Prelude" in Black Light: Roulette War

The Director

The Fixer

"Owned" in Black Light: Roulette Rematch

The Enforcer

The Soldier

The Hacker

The Bookie

The Cleaner

The Player

The Gatekeeper

Alpha Mountain

Hero

Rebel

Warrior

Vegas Underground Mafia Romance

King of Diamonds

Mafia Daddy

Jack of Spades

Ace of Hearts

Joker's Wild

His Queen of Clubs

Dead Man's Hand

Wild Card

Contemporary

Daddy Rules Series

Fire Daddy

Hollywood Daddy

Stepbrother Daddy

Master Me Series

Her Royal Master

Her Russian Master

Her Marine Master

Yes, Doctor

Double Doms Series

Theirs to Punish

Theirs to Protect

Holiday Feel-Good

Scoring with Santa

Saved

Other Contemporary

Black Light: Valentine Roulette

Black Light: Roulette Redux

Black Light: Celebrity Roulette

Black Light: Roulette War

Black Light: Roulette Rematch

Punishing Portia (written as Darling Adams)

The Professor's Girl

Safe in his Arms

Paranormal

Two Marks Series

Untamed

Tempted

Desired

Enticed

Wolf Ranch Series

Rough

Wild

Feral

Savage

Fierce

Ruthless

Wolf Ridge High Series

Alpha Bully

Alpha Knight

Bad Boy Alphas Series

Alpha's Temptation

Alpha's Danger

Alpha's Prize

Alpha's Challenge

Alpha's Obsession

Alpha's Desire

Alpha's War

Alpha's Mission

Alpha's Bane

Alpha's Secret

Alpha's Prey

Alpha's Sun

Shifter Ops

Alpha's Moon

Alpha's Vow

Alpha's Revenge

Alpha's Fire

Alpha's Rescue

Alpha's Command

Midnight Doms

Alpha's Blood

His Captive Mortal

All Souls Night

Alpha Doms Series

The Alpha's Hunger

The Alpha's Promise

The Alpha's Punishment

The Alpha's Protection (Dirty Daddies)

Other Paranormal

The Winter Storm: An Ever After Chronicle

Sci-Fi

Zandian Masters Series

His Human Slave

His Human Prisoner

Training His Human

His Human Rebel

His Human Vessel

His Mate and Master

Zandian Pet

Their Zandian Mate

His Human Possession

Zandian Brides

Night of the Zandians

Bought by the Zandians

Mastered by the Zandians

Zandian Lights

Kept by the Zandian

Claimed by the Zandian

Stolen by the Zandian

Other Sci-Fi

The Hand of Vengeance

Her Alien Masters

ABOUT VANESSA VALE

A USA Today bestseller, Vanessa Vale writes tempting romance with unapologetic bad boys who don't just fall in love, they fall hard. Her books have sold over one million copies. She lives in the American West where she's always finding inspiration for her next story. While she's not as skilled at social media as her kids, she loves to interact with readers.

vanessavaleauthor.com

- facebook.com/vanessavaleauthor
- instagram.com/vanessa_vale_author
- amazon.com/Vanessa-Vale/e/B00PGB3AXC
- bookbub.com/profile/vanessa-vale
- tiktok.com/@vanessavaleauthor

ABOUT RENEE ROSE

USA TODAY BESTSELLING AUTHOR RENEE ROSE loves a dominant, dirty-talking alpha hero! She's sold over two million copies of steamy romance with varying levels of kink. Her books have been featured in USA Today's *Happily Ever After* and *Popsugar*. Named Eroticon USA's Next Top Erotic Author in 2013, she has also won *Spunky and Sassy's* Favorite Sci-Fi and Anthology author, *The Romance Reviews* Best Historical Romance, and *has* hit the *USA Today* list over a dozen times with her Chicago Bratva, Bad Boy Alpha and Wolf Ranch series, as well as various anthologies.

Renee loves to connect with readers!
www.reneeroseromance.com
renee@reneeroseromance.com

- facebook.com/reneeroseromance
- twitter.com/reneeroseauthor
- instagram.com/reneeroseromance
- amazon.com/Renee-Rose/e/B008ASoFT0
- bookbub.com/authors/renee-rose
- tiktok.com/@authorreneerose

Printed in Great Britain
by Amazon